A Bramble House Christmas

A Bramble House Christmas

C.J. Carmichael

for Jennifer
Welcome to Bramble House!

C J Carmichael

TULE
PUBLISHING

ISBN: 978-1-944925-25-3

Dedication

With love to my life partner, Mike Fitzpatrick, who, this Christmas, will also become my husband.

Chapter One

WILLA FAIRCHILD HADN'T counted on driving through a blizzard on her first night in Montana, but given the way her life had gone the past two-and-a-half years, maybe she should have.

"Are we almost there?"

Her six-year-old son's eyes looked huge reflected in the rearview mirror. Scout, strapped into a booster seat in the back of the rented Ford Escape, obviously found the big storm intimidating, too.

"Fifteen more minutes. I think." Quickly she returned her focus to the road, her shoulders tight, her eyes straining. It was dark and snowy and she had to fight the wind to keep a steady path.

Traveling from Arizona to Montana for Christmas hadn't been Willa's idea. But a very special patient who'd recently passed away had gifted her a three-week stay at Bramble House B&B in Marietta, Montana. And when she'd mentioned the idea to Scout, he'd been excited to travel somewhere new and have a white Christmas for a change.

They were both open to fresh experiences these days, now that Scout had finally—thank you, God—been declared cancer-free.

A gust of wind rattled the car as a semi-truck blasted by her, sending up a cloud of snow as well. For two full seconds she was completely blind. And then she spotted the yellow dotted line again.

Whew.

Their flight from Phoenix to Bozeman had been smooth enough. They were in the rental car line-up when the snow started. By the time they were on the highway, the wind had begun to howl.

Just her luck.

The windshield wipers flapped against the steady on-slaught of snow, yet despite the terrible road conditions, Willa knew she was driving too slowly. A steady stream of vehicles had been passing her since she'd merged onto the interstate. But she'd never driven in a snowstorm before and didn't have the nerve to go faster.

She hunched over the steering wheel, her head aching with tension as another semi overtook her, spewing clouds of snow over her car, causing the Escape—and her—to shudder again.

Thwap, thwap. Seconds later she could see again, and her panic subsided. Blurry fluorescent white letters on a green background appeared like a beacon on the right hand side of the highway. "Marietta 8."

Thank God.

Scout had seen the sign, too. "Only eight more miles, Mom."

"Yup. We'll be there before you know it." Willa was a master at sounding optimistic and cheerful when she felt the exact opposite.

It was a necessary skill to acquire when your son was diagnosed with acute lymphoid leukemia at the age of three-and-a-half years.

Willa snatched another glance at the rearview mirror, this time to check if another vehicle was about to pass. But all she saw was the same pair of large headlights that had been traveling behind her since she'd left the airport. Another chicken driver, like her, who was terrified of the snow, ice and wind?

At least the driver had the good sense to keep a large buffer between them. Willa didn't think she could handle a tailgater tonight.

Another green sign loomed ahead—this one signaling the right hand exit, which would lead them to Marietta. A moment after Willa turned on her indicator light, the vehicle behind her did the same.

It was an interesting coincidence, but one Willa forgot all about as she focused on slowing cautiously, taking the turn safely, then gradually easing back to her cruising speed of forty-five miles an hour.

Thank God they were almost at Marietta, because if anything, the snow seemed to be coming down harder now. Gobs of it were collecting at the base of the wipers. She ought to stop and clear it off—but she could hardly see the lane she was driving in now, let alone the shoulder. It seemed safer to continue with reduced visibility than risk a stop.

Before long they came to the one-mile marker.

Willa could sense her son's anticipation as he leaned forward in his booster seat until his head was almost in line with hers.

"Remember Mom," Scout cautioned. "Don't tell anyone about the cancer."

Her son was tired of being "the boy with leukemia," the kid other boys and girls were scared to play with in case they gave him germs, or hurt him in some other, incalculable way.

"I won't forget." How could she? It was the first and last thought she had every day. *My son is cured. Thank you, God.*

The oncologist had assured her there were no more cancer cells in her son's body. And yet...she couldn't stop studying Scout's face every day, worrying when he looked too pale, or seemed too tired.

She'd thought she would feel so happy the day their ordeal was over.

Instead, she felt drained. Old beyond her years. And very alone.

"I see lights! Look, Mom, through the snow! Isn't it awesome?"

"Sure is." Her muscles relaxed as she spotted the festive

reds, greens and golds glowing in the distance.

Marietta. The Bramble House Bed and Breakfast. Christmas.

The drive—heck the past two-and-a-half years—may have been a nightmare.

But good things awaited them now, surely.

FINN CONRAD PARKED on a side street, killed his lights, and then waited while the woman and her son gathered their luggage and entered the bed and breakfast. From the outside, the three-story Victorian—the largest home on the block and quite possibly in all of Marietta—looked both stately and welcoming.

Fairy lights were strung along the eaves and porch railings and in the large front window, a Christmas tree glittered red, green and gold.

Presumably the Brambles had once been a family of some importance in this town. That they no longer held this position seemed self-evident, given that they had opened their doors to the hospitality trade.

Once the Fairchilds were inside and out of sight, Finn pulled his rented GMC truck into the guest parking lot, snagging an empty spot opposite from where Willa had parked her small SUV. Back here he could see a large garage with what looked like living quarters above. Lights glowed behind the pulled curtains.

He sagged into his headrest, glad the drive was over.

Willa Fairchild's snail-like pace had almost been the death of him. She was either a very nervous driver or she didn't have much experience with winter road conditions. Since he knew where she was heading, he could have passed her. But what if she hit a patch of black ice or something?

It was far from his place to worry about Willa Fairchild. Knowing she had a kid in the car with her, though, changed things.

So he'd followed a safe distance behind them to make sure they didn't run into trouble.

He had so many questions about this woman. After today he added another to the list. What was she doing in Marietta, Montana?

It seemed to be a nice enough town. And Bramble House B&B had made the national spotlight last year when country music star, John Urban, announced on the Jane and Ty Show that he planned to go there for Christmas.

But there were lots of nice towns in this country, with plenty of charming bed and breakfasts. Most of them a hell of a lot easier to get to.

Maybe she had family here. Friends. He supposed he'd find out soon enough.

The clock on his dash clicked forward to eight p.m. He pulled out his phone and found four text messages from his mother. He texted to let her know he'd arrived okay, but didn't answer any of her other questions.

He loved his mother, but she was an exhausting woman,

especially since her divorce from his father two years ago. Every time a light bulb burnt out in her house, she was on the phone to him, wondering what to do. The fact that he lived in Colorado and she in Seattle made no difference.

His mother leaned on his three younger sisters, too, albeit in different ways. Molly, married with two children of her own, bore the brunt of their mother's emotional distress. To her fell the role of listening to their mother's litany of complaints about their dad's desertion, his lack of loyalty to her and the family, his selfishness.

From an early age Molly's twin, Keelin, had used academics as a buffer from their family issues. Now a genetics counselor, Keelin was a veritable workaholic. It was interesting how often the dates of her out-of-town conferences conflicted with family birthdays and holidays. Not that Finn blamed her. Their family could be exhausting.

The baby of the family, Berneen, was still living at home and attending the University of Washington. She was twenty-five years old and still hadn't managed to complete a degree because she kept dropping out. One year it was to start her own jewelry-making business. When that didn't pan out she tried writing and self-publishing a cookbook that netted her all of thirty-five dollars.

Finn suspected his mother enabled Berneen's lack of focus because she didn't want her youngest moving out and leaving her alone.

He glanced at his phone again. Fifteen minutes had

passed. That ought to be enough. He grabbed his duffel bag from the passenger seat, then the bag containing his laptop, camera and sketch pad.

Not for the first time since he'd booked his ticket and accommodation, he wondered if he was making a mistake. Any plan hatched by his mother and Berneen was bound to be suspect. But then he thought about his father, and knew he had to have answers. Shaking his head, he braced for the cold.

Wind slashed snow pellets at his face and he had to shield his eyes in order to see as he dashed along the shoveled walkway to the front entry. Outdoor carpet ran up the stairs, all the way to the massive wood door. A small sign in the window invited him to come inside.

He was greeted with a waft of warm, gingerbread-scented air. Another sign, this one on a table next to an umbrella stand, asked him to remove his boots and leave them on the rack by the door.

The foyer was large, with dark wooden floors and papered walls in a tastefully muted floral pattern. Straight ahead was a gracious, curved staircase, and next to that a Christmas tree that looked about fourteen or fifteen feet tall. Not the red, green and gold lit tree he'd seen from the street, this one had blue and gold lights. A closer look revealed ornaments that all had something to do with cowboys, ranching or mountains.

As he reached out to examine a beautiful wooden carving

of a black quarter horse, a man in a hunter green parka, hands encased in thick gloves, emerged from the back of the house.

"Hi, there. That's our Montana tree. Eliza has a tree in every room, each one decorated in a unique theme."

"Impressive."

"Hell of a night, isn't it? I'm Marshall McKenzie. My wife, Eliza, and I manage this place, along with her great-aunt Mable."

Finn had never stayed in a bed and breakfast before, but it seemed the staff was a lot more informal and friendly than at a hotel. He shook the man's proffered hand. "Finn—" he paused only slightly before adding, "Knightly."

"You're the book illustrator from Colorado?"

Finn nodded. This Marshall guy was tall, and even with his big coat, he had the look of being trim and in good shape. From his tanned skin, Finn guessed he was into outdoor sports. Given the location, he probably liked to ski.

"Well, this blizzard will be nothing new for you," Marshall said. "We just had a woman and her son check in from Phoenix. Poor lady was pretty frazzled after her drive from the Bozeman airport."

I know. "The roads weren't that bad. No ice, at least. And the fresh snow will be good for the ski hills."

The answering gleam in Marshall's eyes told Finn he'd guessed correctly. "You ski?"

"Sure do. Eliza and I enjoy snowshoeing too. Wish I

didn't have to work tomorrow. Did you bring your equipment with you?" Marshall glanced at Finn's bags, which he'd left next to the shoe rack.

"No, my skis are in rough shape. I've been meaning to buy new ones, boots, too. Anyway, I plan to spend most of my time taking photos and sketching for my next book."

"Working through Christmas?"

Finn shrugged. "Tight deadline. But I've got three weeks so I hope to do a little skiing eventually."

"Cool. I also work at Montana Wilds Adventure Company. We've got a sweet pre-Christmas sale going on at our store on Main Street. Pop in sometime and I'll show you your options. You can rent or buy. Whatever you prefer."

"I might just do that."

"Okay. Well, I should get out there and do some more shoveling. Eliza will be here shortly to show you to your room."

He no sooner said that, than a tall blonde wearing skinny jeans and a baggy red sweater decorated with a Santa face, emerged carrying a tray of cookies, clearly the source of the delicious aroma that filled this house.

"Hi! Finn Knightly?" She didn't wait for him to reply. "I'm Eliza McKenzie. Here, try a cookie. Santa's been experimenting with his recipe and I think he's finally got it exactly right."

Speechless, Finn stared from her pretty, bright-eyed face, to the over-the-top tacky sweater, to the plate of sugar-dusted, ginger-scented cookies.

He took a cookie. Bit into it. Wow. Flavors exploded, then melted into his mouth. Brown sugar, molasses, cinnamon, cloves, butter…lots of creamy butter. And ginger.

He glanced behind himself, expecting Marshall to reach for a cookie, too, but the other man had gone outside, presumably to deal with the still-falling snow.

"Did you say Santa baked these?"

Eliza laughed. "Yes. He's staying with us over the holidays. Aren't we lucky?"

Finn decided to roll with it. "What about Mrs. Claus?"

"Unfortunately her flight out of the North Pole was cancelled."

Of course it was. Finn smiled. "Is my room ready?"

"It is. Let me give you a quick tour and then I'll take you up."

She led him through open French doors to a large room with comfortable-looking brown leather furniture arranged around a massive fireplace where several logs burned merrily.

"This is the sitting room. You'll usually find refreshments here, as well as a bit of company, if you're in the mood for a visit, though it's quiet now." She set the tray of cookies next to a bowl of apples on the sideboard.

On the opposite wall, by the window, was a tree decorated with gold, green and red lights. It was the tree he'd spotted from the street. What he hadn't been able to see from a distance were the dozens of tiny, silver picture frames hanging from the branches.

He touched one of them. It was a black and white photograph of a woman in her twenties or thirties, taken around the turn of the century. On the back was engraved, *Elizabeth Bramble – 1877 to 1954.*

"I'm the Bramble family historian," Eliza explained. "I've got miniature portraits here dating back to Henry and May Bell—who were the first Brambles to settle in Marietta."

"So they built this house?"

"They did." She indicated that he should follow her for the rest of the tour.

On the other side of the foyer was the library with a literary-themed Christmas tree. "This is the perfect place to read or play games in the afternoon. My great-aunt, Mable, likes to sit here in the morning and early evening, so it's restricted to family at those times."

Finn wondered what this great-aunt thought about her home being opened to guests and other strangers. "Has this house been operated as a bed and breakfast for long?"

"Just a few years." Eliza's pale skin colored and abruptly she turned and led the way to the room at the back corner of the house, behind the sitting room.

"This is where we serve our breakfast, from seven to nine. In between times, if you're hungry, we usually have a pot of soup on the stove in the kitchen."

He peeked into the darkened room, where a large wooden table was already set with linens, old-fashioned china and gleaming silver. The tree here was somewhat smaller than the others. "Does it have a theme?"

"It's our copper tree, celebrating Marietta's mining history."

"So a total of four trees. Cool."

"Actually, there are five. We have a tree decorated with a baking theme in the kitchen, but unfortunately, due to health code restrictions, that room is off limits to our guests."

"Except for Santa."

"But even he has to wear a hair net and wash his hands."

She pointed out the restrooms next, then her great-aunt's suite on the other side of the kitchen, which was another off-limits area. Finally Finn grabbed his bags and they headed up the grand staircase to the second level, where Finn knew from the website were four large guest suites.

"You're in the Brown room." Eliza opened the door to a room with a four poster bed. A cozy armchair with a footstool sat in one corner. A desk in the other.

"This looks perfect."

Just as he was about to step inside, the door to the room opposite his opened, and out stepped Willa Fairchild, wearing a thick, cream-colored robe, her long, chestnut-colored hair piled high on her head.

This was the closest he'd been to her, and he was surprised by how young she looked. She had very pale skin, generous lips, and an off-center small mole on her chin. Her dark-lashed, brown eyes had a vulnerable quality that also caught him off guard.

He supposed he'd expected them to have a calculating, if not mercenary, gleam.

But she was, in fact, perfectly lovely.

"Hi Willa," Eliza said. "Is everything okay?"

"The room is so comfy. Thanks so much for setting up the extra rollaway bed, but my son is hungry. I thought I'd grab him an apple...?" Her gaze slipped from Eliza to Finn.

He thought her eyes widened slightly. Did she recognize him from the airport? But he'd been so careful to keep his distance. He proffered his hand.

"Hi, I'm Finn Knightly, from Colorado. Just got in myself. Quite a storm out there."

"I'll say. I'm Willa Fairchild from Phoenix. The worst I have to deal with at home is a heavy downpour."

"And I'm Scout." Willa's son came to the door, already dressed in pajamas. He, too, had pale skin and his very short hair was the same color as his mother.

"Hey, Scout. How do you like Montana so far?" Finn asked.

"I've never seen snow before. I took some up to my room but it's melted already. Tomorrow we're going to make a snowman, right Mom?"

She put a hand on his head and smiled. "You bet. But first, we need to sleep. You pick out a book and I'll be right back with that apple."

"Okay." Obediently he slipped back into the room.

"Good kid," Finn commented. He couldn't remember his own niece or nephew ever saying "okay" to anything Molly requested them to do. At least not the first time she asked.

"Grab a few cookies while you're down there," Eliza suggested to Willa. "Fresh from the oven about fifteen minutes ago."

"Santa's secret recipe," Finn added, earning a smile from Eliza and a puzzled, over-the-shoulder glance from Willa.

"I hope you like the room," Eliza said, opening the door wider. "There's a full bathroom, including a jetted spa tub, through that door."

"I'm sure it will be great." Finn was still watching Willa, though, who'd just disappeared around the curve in the stairwell.

She wasn't anything like he'd imagined.

At least now Finn understood why his father had fallen under her spell.

Chapter Two

FINN WAS TIRED. For the past month—ever since his father died—he'd been having bad dreams and restless nights.

His father's death had been an unexpected blow, since no one in the family even knew he'd been diagnosed with pancreatic cancer. It was so typical of his father that he hadn't wanted to worry anyone. Instead, his dad had hired private care and lived out his last weeks in his Phoenix condo with only his golfing buddies to keep him company.

It was some comfort to know that at least his father had been truly happy these past few years, enjoying his biggest passions in life, golfing and woodworking.

Still, it had hurt to have his last communication from his father come in the form of a letter. "I love you, son and I know you love me, too. I hope you're not angry with me for handling things this way. I've always hated having people fuss over me, and that's exactly what your sisters would have done. And I could hardly have told you about my illness without telling them. I had a good life—especially these last years—and I wish you the best with yours. You know I've always been proud of your talent and your career. I hope you find more than that one day. Love and companionship can be wonderful things—I'm only sorry your mother and I didn't set a better example for you children on that score…"

The letter had gone on for another two pages. Tears had been running down Finn's face by the time he was done with it.

Shortly after that Molly had called. Then Berneen. And finally his mother.

Three nurses had helped his father through his illness. In his will he'd left two of them five thousand dollars. The third nurse he'd left fifty thousand.

Fifty!

Something fishy must have been going on. As the only son and the eldest child, he was expected to get to the bottom of it.

So here he was. In Marietta, Montana, hoping to find answers that would satisfy his sisters as well as himself.

At six-thirty in the morning Finn got out of the bed, which had been extremely comfortable. From the window, in the murky pre-dawn light, he could see it was still snowing. At least the wind had calmed. The house was eerily quiet, in fact.

Finn dragged himself into the shower, and after that, he shaved and dressed in warm layers, suspecting most of his day would be spent out of doors. It was just shy of seven when he left his room.

All was quiet on the second floor. He paused to glance up toward the third floor. Again from the website he knew there were two big suites up there. One was living quarters for family members—he presumed this was for Eliza and Marshall. The other, the Big Sky Suite, had been rented out by country music star John Urban last year.

He wondered why Willa hadn't booked the bigger space for herself and her son. She must be feeling flush, after all, given the money she'd inherited from his father's estate.

Downstairs, no one was present, except for a dog sleeping by the fire in the sitting room. About the size of a small lab, it had the sharp ears and eyes of a German Shepherd, but the quiet disposition of an area rug. After sleepily raising his head, to give Finn the once-over, the dog sank back into his nap.

Finn went to make friends, checking the tag on the collar as he did so. "Hi, Ace. Looks like you have the best seat in the house." Finn straightened, then moved on. The door to the breakfast room was open, so he went inside.

The table was set, as it had been last night. On a long sideboard were thermoses of hot water and coffee. He helped himself to a mug of the coffee, then headed to the window again. This time he was looking out the back of the house with a view of the carriage house and what was probably a vegetable or flower garden in the summer. A flash of green at the far corner of the garden caught his eye, and he moved closer for a better view.

The green was Scout Fairchild's jacket. The boy was rolling a ball of snow, which was growing noticeably larger with each rotation. A moment later his mother came into view. Willa was wearing a white jacket, with a fur-lined hood pulled up over her head, red mittens, and a loosely looped red scarf.

Willa was also rolling a ball of snow—this one about twice as big as her son's.

Finn drank his coffee—which was damn good—and watched as Willa picked up her snowball and placed it on top of an even larger ball that must have been made earlier. Next Scout added his own effort—the head. And thus a snowman was born.

Willa unwove her scarf and donated it to the snowman. Scout added three brown, round, flat objects for buttons, and a carrot nose. Mother and son stood back to contemplate for a few moments. Then Willa broke two dead branches off a nearby aspen and added arms.

Finally they seemed satisfied. Willa took out her phone and snapped a "selfie" with herself, her son and the snowman. Then she took a picture with just Scout and the snowman.

It should have been a heartwarming scene. Since this was Scout's first encounter with snow, undoubtedly this was also the first time he'd made a snowman, too. But the mother's and son's expressions were so serious.

He must have been concentrating on the outdoor scene

harder than he'd realized, because when the connecting door from the kitchen opened, he was startled. Eliza entered with a bowl of fruit salad, which she placed on the sideboard. Today she was wearing black leggings, short boots, and another God-awful Christmas sweater, this one featuring a reindeer with a red pompom for a nose.

"Good morning. I hope you slept well?"

Before he could answer, an elderly woman with regal posture entered the room and claimed the chair with the best view of the snow-covered garden. Her gray hair was piled into a sizeable bun, and she was dressed in a tweed skirt and cashmere sweater.

"This is Finn Knightly, Aunt Mable. He's the children's book illustrator I was telling you about."

Eliza's introduction was met with barely concealed disinterest on the older woman's face. "Could you be so good as to pour me some tea, Eliza?"

"Of course."

Finn took a seat to Mable's right. Mable's pursed mouth, and her short, jerky head movements made him think of on owl. A very old, very tall, very thin owl. "That was quite the storm last night."

"Snow and wind." Mable shrugged. "What do you expect when you're in Montana in December?"

"Fair enough." Finn met Eliza's apologetic expression with an unworried grin.

Willa and her son showed up then, cheeks and finger-tips

tinged with pink. "Oh, that coffee smells good." Willa went straight to the sideboard. "Scout would you like some hot cocoa?"

"Yes, please."

"So what did you think of the snow?" Finn asked.

"It's very cold." Scout shivered, just thinking about it.

"What did you expect?" Mable asked. It seemed to be her stock comment for the morning.

Scout shrugged. "I thought it would be more like whipped cream. And not so heavy."

"Did you taste it?" Finn wondered.

"I hope not," Willa said.

Scout gave her a sheepish smile. "It wasn't sweet at all. It didn't taste like anything."

"Of course it didn't. Snow is simply crystalized water," Mable said.

"But wouldn't it be awesome if it *did* taste like whipped cream?" Eliza was back, this time with a tray containing a basket of scones that smelled and looked freshly baked.

"What a treat," Willa murmured. "Does it matter where we sit?"

"Anywhere you like. Marshall and I will be joining you once the frittata is out of the oven. Is there anything special Scout would like? We can make him a boiled, or fried egg. We also have boxed cereal if he prefers."

"Oh, don't worry about Scout. He's used to hos—"

"—Mom." Scout scowled at his mother.

Willa brought her hand to her mouth. "Sorry. I shouldn't answer for him. Is there anything special you'd like, Scout?"

The little boy shook his head, but at that point Finn was no longer following the conversation. His gaze was riveted to the ring on Willa's right hand, a one carat, Montana sapphire that he'd last seen in his mother's jewelry box.

He wasn't the only one who noticed.

"That's a lovely ring, dear," Mable commented. "It reminds me very much of a ring my great-grandmother is wearing in the only photo we still have of her. Would you mind allowing me to take a closer look?"

Finn frowned at this. One carat Montana sapphires weren't exactly a dime a dozen. And this one had a unique setting. Of course Mable was old. Probably she was mistaken.

Willa slipped the ring off her finger so she could pass it to Mable. "It was a gift from a patient of mine. I'm a nurse. An RN."

"A rather extravagant gift," Mable murmured, as she held the ring this way, then that. "Extraordinary," she added before returning the ring.

"Do your patients often fall in love with you and shower you with expensive gifts?" Finn asked, hoping his tone was light.

Willa quickly replaced it on her finger. "It wasn't like

that. My patient was a very sweet man in his early sixties. He had pulled the ring out of a drawer one evening and was just sitting in bed, looking at it. I commented on how lovely it was. I had never seen a Montana sapphire before—didn't even know there was such a thing. My patient seemed surprised that I liked it. Apparently he'd given it to his wife as a wedding present but she hadn't liked it and had never even worn it."

Mable clucked with disapproval.

"He and his wife were since divorced. Their daughters had never cared for the ring either, they said it was too old-fashioned. As he knew he was dying. he said he wanted to give it to me. That it would make him happy to know someone was wearing it and enjoying it."

Finn struggled to keep his composure. It was possible she was telling the truth. But if so, it meant his father had given her fifty thousand dollars *and* a very valuable ring. And yet she sat there all wide-eyed and innocent, as if she had nothing in the world to be ashamed of. "That's quite the generous patient you had."

"In my profession you meet all kinds, but this man was such a kind and generous soul. I didn't have the heart to turn down his gift, even though I felt uncomfortable accepting it."

Finn wondered what she would say if she knew she was sitting with her patient's son right now. He was almost tempted to reveal the connection, to demand she tell him everything she knew about Greg Conrad—and why he'd left her fifty thousand dollars, not to mention that ring.

But chances were she'd only clam up. So he took a drink of coffee instead. And a moment later Eliza and her husband emerged from the kitchen.

Marshall went around the table, dishing out the frittata, while Eliza passed the fruit salad, and then the scones and preserves.

The large table had been made up for seven, so once Eliza and Marshall had finished serving and taken their seats, one chair remained unoccupied.

"Is someone else joining us?" Finn asked.

"Oh, that's for Santa," Eliza said. "But he said he's too busy getting ready for the Marietta Christmas Stroll to eat."

"Did you say Santa?" Willa asked.

"Yes. He's booked into the Red room. He baked the cookies I mentioned last night."

"Um." Scout looked uncomfortable. "You know there's no such thing as a real Santa, right?"

"Don't tell Kris Krinkles that. He hates to be told he's imaginary." Something out the window caught Eliza's attention then. "Look at all the chickadees on the snowman."

They all turned to the window and it was true. A half dozen little birds with black caps and plump white bellies were flitting around the snowman Willa and Scout had made that morning.

"What did you use for buttons?" Finn asked, noticing that they seemed to be the big attraction for the birds.

Scout and his mother exchanged a guilty look, and then Willa said. "Sorry, we didn't know they'd been specially baked by Santa."

"Well, the birds are sure enjoying them," Mable said placidly.

WILLA WAS BEGINNING to wonder if coming to Marietta had been such a good idea, after all. Scout seemed rather disappointed after his first experience with snow. And the people here—while they were friendly enough—made her feel a bit uncomfortable.

That sharp-eyed old woman had been so strange about her ring. And then the hunk from Colorado—Finn something or other—had appeared to be joking when he asked about patients falling in love with her. But she'd heard the disapproving note in his voice.

Maybe she *shouldn't* have accepted the ring. But it had made poor Mr. Conrad happy. And it was definitely too late now to give it back.

At least Eliza seemed nice, and fairly normal. But those sweaters. And the way she kept talking about Santa, as if he truly was a guest at the B&B and had baked those cookies last night.

She spread huckleberry preserves over her scone and took

a bite. *Oh, my*. At least the food here was amazing.

"So what are you and Scout planning for today?" Finn asked her.

He sounded friendly enough now, but she answered cautiously. "We'll probably do a little shopping in the morning and hit the Marietta Christmas Stroll later in the afternoon."

Scout was looking forward to the hay wagon ride. And she wanted to get his photo with Santa—it would be the first in two years that wouldn't be taken in a hospital.

"Make sure you pick up your Marietta Stroll buttons at one of the downtown shops," Eliza advised them. "The button is only three dollars and it gains you admittance to all the events, including the hayride and the petting zoo."

She turned to Finn. "Are you planning to take in the Christmas Stroll, as well?"

"Definitely. I'll be taking lots of photos for my latest project. The more Christmassy, the better."

Marshall caught Willa's eye. "Finn is an illustrator of children's books."

"How interesting." So he was here for work. Somehow she felt more comfortable about him now that she knew that. "Do you create the illustrations from photographs?"

"Sometimes. Or sketches. But when the temps go below freezing, that's problematic." He flexed his fingers, which would no doubt freeze if he tried to sit outside with a sketchbook.

"Tell us more about your current project." Eliza's eyes

were bright with interest. "We've had writers stay with us before, but never an illustrator."

Finn looked a little uncomfortable, as if he didn't enjoy being the center of attention. "The story I'm working on now takes place in a small town at Christmas. That's really all I'm at liberty to say. I don't write the stories. I just make the pictures. In this case I'll be making watercolors based on my photos, then when I'm back at my studio, I'll scan them into my computer and finish them up on Photoshop."

"What other books have you worked on?" Over the years she and Scout had read countless stories...most of them during one of his interminable hospital stays. "Maybe Scout and I have read one of your books."

"Too many to name, really. I work with more than one author."

"What's your last name again?"

He hesitated. "Knightly."

"Hm." She tried really hard, but couldn't recall seeing Finn Knightly on a book jacket.

"Don't feel bad. All the glory goes to the authors. Hardly anyone remembers the name of the guy who does the illustrations."

"It's the same for us nurses. All the glory goes to the doctors."

He smiled briefly at that, and she had the oddest sensation of familiarity. As if she'd met him before.

But she would not have forgotten meeting a man as

good-looking as Finn Knightly.

She noticed him staring at her ring, again, and realized she'd been twirling it with her thumb. She always felt self-conscious when people commented on it. She'd considered putting it away for safekeeping. But Greg Conrad had asked her to wear it. To enjoy it. And to think of him now and again.

So that's what she was doing.

"If you're heading downtown," Finn said, "maybe I could walk with you and your son? I hear Main Street is very picturesque."

The invitation surprised her. She'd had the distinct impression that he disapproved of her for some unknown reason. Maybe she'd misread him. She was about to tell him sure, when Mable Bramble stepped in front of her, brandishing a small, silver-framed portrait.

"Look at this," she insisted. "This is my great-grandmother, May Bell Bramble."

Willa took the small ornament in her hands. During their tour of the B&B last night, Eliza had pointed out the Bramble Family Christmas tree in the sitting room. This looked like one of the ornaments that had been hanging from its branches.

The woman in the black and white photo was unsmiling, but handsome. She was posed with her chin resting on her left hand.

And there it was. Plain as day.

Willa's spine tingled eerily. The ring on this woman's finger was an exact replica of the one Greg Conrad had given her.

Chapter Three

D URING BREAKFAST FINN'S phone had vibrated continually with text messages from his mother and younger sister Berneen. In his room he finally had a chance to read them.

HAVE YOU MET HER YET?
WHAT'S SHE LIKE?
CAN YOU SEND PICS?

Finn didn't answer any of them. He was pissed off. What did they expect, that he would be able to drag the truth out of Willa Fairchild the moment he met her? If only it could be that easy. But if she had somehow taken advantage of their father, the minute she found out he was Greg Conrad's son, she would undoubtedly clam up.

Then not only would Finn never know what had possessed his father to leave her so much money—*plus* the ring, but he would also lose his chance to talk to the person who had been with his father when he died.

He knew Molly and Keelin also felt guilty about not being there for their dad. Not just at the time of his death, but for the entire two years since he'd moved to Phoenix after the divorce.

But their father had made so few demands on them. And whenever Finn talked to him on the phone, he sounded so happy. He had buddies to golf with, spare time for his woodworking. "And I love the climate," his dad had said, almost every time Finn called. "After thirty-five years in Seattle, I don't miss the rain one bit."

Unsaid, but probably equally true, was the fact that after thirty-five years of being nagged and complained at, he didn't miss his ex-wife one bit either.

Finn's mother, however, was another story.

Her divorce had not freed her, as it had done for his father. It had unhinged her.

No matter how often Finn called, it was never enough. And yet she always had exactly the same things to say during every one of their conversations. Their father had deserted her. He probably had another woman "stashed away somewhere." She'd given him her best years, and for what?

The tirade had only ended with his father's death. At which time his mother had become obsessed with this nurse who'd been left such an inappropriate amount of money considering she'd known Greg Conrad for only six weeks.

The obvious conclusion was that the nurse had somehow conned or manipulated their dad when he was in a weak and vulnerable position.

But now that Finn had met Willa, he wasn't convinced.

She seemed like a kind and caring person—but there was something *not quite right* about her and her son.

Did it have something to do with her relationship with his father?

Finn was convinced he could only find the answers he needed in one way. By becoming her friend.

DESPITE BEING BUNDLED in their warm coats and mittens, Willa and Scout looked chilled to the bone as they walked along Court Street. Their hands were shoved deep into their pockets, and their shoulders were hunched under their jackets. It was only a few degrees below freezing. But he supposed if you were from Arizona, it would be a shock.

"I bet you're sorry now you gave your scarf to Frosty."

Willa laughed. "You read my mind. I was just thinking I should buy another one. And maybe a really warm sweater, as well."

"I bet hot cocoa would warm us up," Scout said helpfully.

"I hear the one they serve at the Copper Mountain Chocolate Shop is exceptional," Finn said. "That was going to be my first stop."

"Excellent idea. We can buy our Christmas Stroll buttons there, too."

Willa glanced at him. Her eyes were bright and the cold had turned her lips a deep crimson. A flake of snow landed briefly on the tip of her nose, then melted. She had a very adorable nose.

If his father had fallen for this women, well, Finn couldn't really blame him.

They walked by the library where a group of workers were busy stringing lights onto one of the stately evergreen trees that grew in the extensive grounds. The local fire truck was pulled up to one of the tallest of the trees, the ladder extended to reach the very top of what looked like a thirty-or forty-foot tree.

"Wow, I'd like to climb that ladder," Scout said.

Alarm flashed in Willa's eyes. "When you're older, maybe you can be a fireman."

"You mean if I don't get into the NHL?"

"It's good to have a back-up plan," Finn agreed. "Do you play hockey in Phoenix?"

"Mom hasn't even let me take skating lessons yet. But I've watched a lot of hockey games on TV. I think I'd be good at it."

"We'll get to the skating lessons." Willa sighed. "Eventually."

"I've heard there's a skating pond around here. I could give Scout his first lesson." The offer just seemed to spring out, before Finn had a chance to consider the wisdom of it. Learning a bit more about Willa was one thing. Fostering a friendship with her son, was another.

Yet he hadn't had an ulterior motive in mind when he'd mentioned the skating lessons. So maybe it was okay.

As they made the right hand turn onto Main Street, suddenly the sidewalks were teeming with people. Right in front of them a man and two women in period dress straight out of a Charles Dickens' novel, were singing *Let it Snow!*

All three of them stopped to watch and listen. Automatically Finn reached for his Nikon. He photographed the carolers and then took shots up and down Main Street.

The pictures on the website hadn't done the town justice. The solid fronts of nineteenth century western-style buildings were beautifully maintained, and all the business owners had gotten into the spirit and decorated for Christmas with sparkling lights and cedar wreaths.

When he turned to the west, he was able to get some shots of the stately courthouse, with snow-covered Copper Mountain rising behind it. He'd have to come back at sunrise one day. The lighting would be fantastic.

Turning around, he adjusted his camera until he had Willa and her son in the viewfinder. They'd strolled ahead to the toy store and had joined a group of children gazing wide-eyed at a front window display that was a simulation of Santa's workshop, right down to a fake fireplace, and several busy elves apparently putting finishing touches on everything from a railway set to a beautiful porcelain doll.

Finn took shots. Dozens of them. Zooming in, he let Scout's face fill the screen, catching the looks of awe in his widened eyes.

Then he turned the camera lens on Willa. She wasn't

looking at the toys, but at her son, with the oddest expression, somewhere between loving and sad. He was reminded of how the mother and son had appeared to him when they were building their snowman, earlier.

What was their story?

And what had happened to Scout's dad? Neither one of them had mentioned the man, even though it was Christmas, a time when most fathers would want to spend time with their children.

Finn slipped his camera back into its case, then crossed the street just as Scout asked his mother if they could go inside the toy store.

"Maybe after we get some hot cocoa," she suggested.

"The chocolate shop is two blocks down," Finn said.

"Can I run?"

Again that look of caution flashed over Willa's face, so fast Finn might have missed it, except that he'd noticed she often had this reaction when her son suggested anything on the boisterous side.

"Better not. It's too crowded. You might knock someone over."

Delicious smells wafted out of a tiny bakery next to the bank. A line-up had formed stretching out to the street. Things weren't much better when they reached Copper Mountain Chocolates where they had to wait fifteen minutes to be served.

"My treat," Finn insisted when it was time to pay. He

took the cups from the server and passed them back to Willa and her son. The three of them lucked into chairs at a small table near the back of the shop.

"I hope this lives up to its rep," Finn said. His first sip gave him his answer.

Willa sampled hers at the same time. Her eyebrows went up. "This is incredible. It's like chocolate and whipped cream got married."

"Add a hint of vanilla and maybe a tiny bit of cinnamon, and I think you've got it." A tall, pretty woman, her thick, red hair braided over one shoulder, came up beside them. From her copper-colored apron it was clear that she worked here.

"Hi, I'm Sage. I'm sorry for the wait. I hope the cocoa is worth it."

"It's great," Scout assured her, his serious demeanor at odds with the whipped cream mustache he was now sporting.

"Whew, glad to know I haven't lost my touch. So where are you folks from?"

"Colorado," Finn offered.

"My son and I are from Phoenix. We're all staying at the Bramble Inn for the holidays."

"How nice! My mother was a Bramble, so I know the B&B well. How are Aunt Mable and cousin Eliza treating you all?"

Before either Finn or Willa could answer, Scout piped up

with, "Your Aunt Mable is kind of grouchy sometimes."

"Scout!" Willa looked embarrassed.

"That's okay." Sage laughed. "When I was a kid I used to be scared when Mom took us to have tea with our great-aunt. She's a throwback to another era, and very proud of the family's English heritage. So, are the three of you going to participate in the lighting festival later? I notice you don't have your Marietta Stroll buttons yet."

"We meant to pick some up," Willa said.

"Great." Sage pulled three from one of the pockets in her apron. "Here you go. Maybe I'll see you at the lighting ceremony. I'll be there with my husband and our two children. Our eldest, Savannah, is about your age, Scout."

"A girl?" Scout didn't look impressed. "Do you have a boy?"

"Yes, but Braden is just a baby."

"Well. Maybe I can play with Savannah, then."

"I'll introduce you," Sage promised. Then she dipped her hand into a different pocket and pulled out a miniature chocolate Christmas tree. "Is it okay if I give this to your son?"

"That's very kind." Willa nodded to Scout that he could accept the gift.

"Thank you!" Scout beamed. "This is a really good chocolate shop, Mom."

"It is, isn't it? I think I'm beginning to understand why Mr. Conrad liked this town so much."

Finn immediately went on alert. "Mr. Conrad?"

"He's the patient who left me this ring." Willa twirled it self-consciously on her finger. "One night when he was having trouble sleeping I asked if there was anything on his bucket list he regretted not doing. Sky-diving or something like that. He laughed and said he hadn't been much for adventure or travel. But he did wish he'd made the time to visit Marietta, Montana."

"This is going to sound crazy, but before he died, he actually booked the room at the B&B for Scout and me."

Finn knew this much, as the trip had been included in the will. "Sounds like this man had a lot of sleepless nights. Was he in a lot of pain?"

"I'm afraid so."

Finn's throat dried up. For a few seconds he couldn't breathe.

"Of course I tried to make him as comfortable as possible."

Finally Finn recovered his voice. "Did this guy have family?"

"Yes. But he'd just gone through an ugly divorce, so he didn't talk about them much." She hesitated. "He had children. I'd hear him speaking with them on the phone occasionally, but they never came to visit. To be fair, he didn't tell them he was sick and dying."

"Did you ask him why?" Finn managed to ask, leaning intently over the table for the answer.

"I did ask but his answer wasn't satisfactory. He said he didn't want to be a burden. That the divorce had already caused the family enough grief."

Finn stared into his mug, infinitely saddened and disappointed with the answer. He had so many more questions to ask, but Willa had turned to her son who was clearly bored of the conversation.

Chapter Four

I T HAD BEEN a long time since a man her age had paid much attention to Willa, so she wasn't sure if she was reading the signals she was getting from Finn Knightly correctly. There were times when she was certain he was attracted to her.

He didn't go so far as to flirt—but maybe that was because Scout was with her.

And yet, other times she felt him studying her with what felt like complete detachment, perhaps even a bit of animosity.

But that didn't make sense.

She was just so out of practice when it came to men that she was hopeless.

So when they were finished with their cocoas and Finn said he was going off on his own to take some more photos, she was actually relieved.

But only for a moment. And then she was disappointed. Because she'd enjoyed having him around and she had so much she still wanted to ask him. They'd spent hours together and she didn't even know where he'd gone to school, if he'd grown up in Colorado…or if he was currently in a relationship.

And yes, that last question was the one she was most curious about.

So, she watched him head off to the historic Graff Hotel with some regret, then shook it off and gave in to Scout's desire to go back to the toy store. They lingered for almost an hour, Willa vastly relieved when Scout was most fascinated by the two toys and the book she'd already purchased for him and hidden in her luggage.

After that, they wandered through a few more stores. She found a couple sweaters she liked and managed to buy them in a two-for-one deal. She also bought a scarf for herself and a fleece sweatshirt for Scout.

They stopped for sandwiches at the Java Café, and as they were leaving, someone called out, "Willa! Scout!"

It was Sage from the chocolate shop, only now she was wearing a wool coat and an ivory-colored toque and had a baby boy bundled in her arms. Beside her was an attractive man in a cowboy hat and sheepskin jacket, holding the hand of a girl who was about four inches taller than Scout.

Before Willa knew it, the family was in front of them and Sage was starting introductions.

"Nice to see you again, Willa and Scout. This is my husband, Dawson O'Dell, and these are our children."

"Nice to meet you." Dawson had the sort of smile that made most women go weak in the knees.

Yet Willa felt immune. There weren't many men who could stir a reaction in her since her son had become ill.

"Hi," Savannah said, next. She had green eyes, just like her father's, and trained them straight at Scout. "I'm Savannah and I'm in second grade. I can ride horses and make really good sandwiches."

"I'm in first grade," Scout admitted, sounding chagrined. He thought a moment then added, "I'm going to be a hockey star when I grow up."

Savannah considered that, then nodded. "Okay. Want to go to the petting zoo?"

Willa glanced at Sage, who gave her a reassuring smile. "It's back by the courthouse. We were just on our way. It would be fun if you and Scout came along."

"All right." Willa couldn't help feeling a little anxious as the kids took off at a run ahead of them. In a crowd like this it would be so easy for them to get lost.

Dawson seemed to be reading her mind. "Don't worry. Savannah knows not to get too far ahead of us. And I've got my eyes on them."

"My husband's a deputy," Sage told her. "It's always safety first with him."

"Ever since I quit riding bucking broncs for a living," he agreed.

"I've never met a cowboy before." Willa was intrigued.

"We're a dime a dozen in this town. Just look around."

There were a lot of men—and women—in cowboy hats.

Willa had assumed they were just for show. But upon closer examination she started to pick out gold rodeo buckles on some of the men—and a couple women, too.

"Marietta started as a mining town," Sage said. "But our economy revolves around ranching and tourism now. Our fall rodeo draws cowboys and tourists from Texas to Alberta and everywhere in between."

The petting zoo had been set up with square straw bales delineating the pens. It was like a giant maze, and again Willa had to quell a panicked fear that she would lose sight of Scout. He and Savannah were dashing from one animal to the next so quickly, she couldn't keep up with them.

Finally she gave up and went to stand with Savannah and Dawson by the miniature goats.

Sage had her arms around her baby, who was too young to take much interest in the animals.

"She's a great mom," Dawson said proudly. "And so are you, I can tell. But honestly, you shouldn't worry about your son. Marietta's a safe place. It's one of the reasons I moved here with my daughter."

Willa took a deep breath. He was right. She had to learn to let go a little where Scout was concerned. "Was there anything else that drew you to Marietta?"

Dawson put an arm around his wife. "Hell, yeah. I was following her. The hard part was convincing her to marry me."

Sage rolled her eyes, but Willa could tell this couple was

tight.

An aching loss rose up in her, something she hadn't let herself feel since months after her husband, Scout's father, had left them. It had been just a few months after Scout's diagnosis. Jeff hadn't been able "to deal" as he put it.

"It's almost time for the lighting procession," Dawson said, noting the time on the town clock.

"I have to take Braden home for his feeding. You and Savannah should stay, though," Sage told her husband.

Willa was sorry to see her leave. "I hope I'll see you again while we're in town."

"You're staying at Bramble House for Christmas?"

When Willa nodded yes, Sage smiled and patted her arm. "Don't worry. You'll see me again. Not least when my youngest sister Callan and I make our annual pilgrimage for Christmas tea with Aunt Mable."

"Callan runs the Carrigan family ranch with her husband Court," Dawson explained. "She's a real pistol. You have to meet her."

"I have two other sisters, but they live far away and won't be home until just a few days before Christmas."

Once Sage was gone, Willa took the opportunity to quiz Dawson about rodeo life, then, about fifteen minutes later, when Scout and Savannah rejoined them, she suggested to Scout that they go back to the B&B and rest up before the hayrides and the lighting procession.

Scout frowned. Then he sidled up to her and whispered.

"I'm better now, Mom. I don't need to rest."

She wished she could trust him on that, but to her eyes he looked pale and tired. "Maybe you don't, but I do."

All was quiet when they arrived at the B&B. There was no sign of Marshall or Eliza...or Finn.

The resident dog, Ace, came to give them a sniff and accepted some pats and scratches, before returning to his post by the fire. The library was closed off to guests. Presumably Mable was having some alone time.

Willa could hear voices coming from the kitchen, but as they weren't hungry and didn't need anything, she just led Scout up the stairs to the Blue room. "Come sit up on the bed with me and I'll put on a Spiderman DVD."

That was enticement enough. The temptation to let Scout watch a lot of TV and movies while he was sick had been great, but she'd resisted, preferring to read books with her son, or play board games when he was feeling strong enough. For Scout, a movie or a TV show was still a big treat.

Willa stayed awake for the first scene. The next thing she knew, Scout was tugging her arm.

"Mom. It's past four o'clock. We don't want to miss the hayride and the Christmas lights and everything."

Willa felt as if she'd been drugged and had to fight to keep her eyes open. "Did you sleep at all?"

"Nah. I told you I wasn't tired."

She sighed. She was constantly underestimating him. In

the past two-and-half years she'd learned how to be a very good mother to a boy who was seriously ill. Now she had to learn to be an equally good mother to a boy who wanted to be active and have fun.

Ten minutes later they were out the door, this time wearing the warmer clothing she'd purchased earlier, plus proudly sporting their Marietta Christmas Stroll buttons.

It was still snowing, but gently, and the sparkling flakes made everything just a little bit prettier. They scrambled into a wagon for the hayride, and then watched the magical lighting ceremony. Everyone in the crowd went "Ah!" as the lights flashed on, first on the decorations strung along the Main Street lamp posts, then on each of the tall evergreens in front of the library and the courthouse.

Willa felt her heart lift at the beauty of it.

Three carolers started singing "O Christmas Tree," and most of the people around them joined in.

The music, the lights, the softly falling snow. It was all so perfect.

Willa squeezed Scout's hand. "What do you think, buddy?"

"I feel like we're in a movie or something."

"Me, too." That was the problem. None of this felt real. "How about we go find Santa Claus?"

"Sure."

She wished Scout sounded more enthusiastic. Last December he'd shared his hospital room with an older boy named William. She guessed William had teased Scout about still believing in Santa Claus, because right after that, Scout had announced he was old enough to know that Santa wasn't real.

Her son's illness had forced him to grow up too fast, in many ways, including facing his own mortality. Willa wished he could have at least been allowed to believe in Santa just a little bit longer.

When they arrived at the historic Graff Hotel, they had to get in line to visit Santa. Fortunately there were teenaged boys and girls dressed as elves to keep them entertained. One of the "elves" was making balloon animals for the waiting children. Another was trying to juggle Christmas ornaments—plastic not glass—with comic results.

Willa glanced around the crowded lobby, looking for Finn, but there was no sign of him.

Perhaps he'd already taken all the photographs he needed and gone back to the B&B.

Twenty minutes later it was Scout's turn to sit on Santa's lap. To please her he smiled when the photographer took their picture, but right after that, he slid to the floor. "Thank you," he said politely, but before he could leave, Santa grasped his hand.

"You're welcome young man. But aren't you going to tell me your name and what you'd like for Christmas?"

He was a very realistic-looking Santa, with twinkly blue eyes and pudgy cheeks. Willa was positive the white beard and hair were real. The velvet of his suit was richly hued and plush, and his boots and belt appeared to be genuine leather.

"That's okay. I gave my mom my list and she probably did her shopping in Phoenix before we left."

Up went Santa's white eyebrows. "So…you're Scout Fairchild, then?"

Scout's face registered shock. "How did you guess?"

"We're staying at the same B&B. Did you like my cookies?"

Scout looked stunned. "I used three for my snowman this morning. I think the birds ate them."

Santa laughed. "Well, I haven't perfected my recipe yet, anyway. I'm going to make some adjustments to the spices next time." He tilted his head to one side. "Are you sure you don't want to ask me for something for Christmas?"

For a second Willa thought her son might do it. She held her breath and hoped. But then he shook his head.

"I already have a lot of toys and books. I only want skates and hockey pads and the next Everyday Sam book. I think my mom will get me those."

"Hm. I bet you're the kind of boy who likes adventures," Santa said. "Am I right about that?"

Scout nodded vigorously. "But I've never had one."

"I bet you also like to help other people. Not just worry about yourself all the time."

Scout's eyes widened, then he nodded again, this time more thoughtfully.

"Okay then, leave it to me Scout. I'll make sure this is a Christmas you never forget."

IT WAS NINE o'clock by the time Willa had her son back to the B&B, where he ate his snack, took a shower, and then sat through several bedtime stories. He could read most of his books himself now—a byproduct of those hours spent in hospital beds—but he still preferred to have Willa read to him at night.

It was a routine Willa cherished, because in so many other ways her son was growing up fast. They'd had to have a rollaway bed brought up to their room, for instance, because he now insisted he was too old to sleep in the same bed as her.

As she tucked him in, she brushed her hand over his new crop of hair, resisting the urge to check his temperature...just to be sure.

"What was your favorite part of the day?"

"The petting zoo," he murmured.

"Savannah seems like a nice girl."

"She's okay. I really liked the puppies. And the little goats."

Willa kissed his cheek. "I'm going downstairs to read so I don't disturb you. I have the monitor with me, so just call out if you need me?"

He groaned, then turned over on his side. She knew he hated when she used the monitor—he was too old! He didn't need that baby stuff—but he was also too tired to argue with her.

So she took her book and the receiver end of the monitor and, leaving the door a little ajar, went out into the hall. Eliza was coming up the stairs carrying an armful of towels.

"Oh, hi. I've left Scout sleeping in our room. I just wanted to check whether any other guests have booked in to the vacant rooms?" She trusted Finn, and if Santa really was staying here, she trusted him too, but she wouldn't leave Scout if strangers were going to be milling around.

"Don't worry, Scout will be fine. We have a woman renting out the mini apartment above the garage—but Whitney is a workaholic, we hardly ever see her. Our only other guest right now is Emma McGregor. She arrived in Marietta a week ago, alone and in her wedding dress."

"That doesn't sound good."

"No, poor thing. She's a lovely girl. But you won't see her often, either. She works long hours at the Graff—plus our local high school varsity football coach has been keeping an eye on her."

Willa's eyebrows went up. "Oh? Is romance in the air?"

"Of course. It's a house specialty. Hasn't anyone warned you?"

Willa laughed, assuming she was joking.

"How did you enjoy the Christmas stroll? Did Scout finally meet Santa?"

"We had an excellent time. And Scout and Santa had

quite the chat." Willa was a little worried about it, though. How was she going to follow through on that promise Santa had made to her son?

In the sitting room Willa settled into a love seat close to the crackling fire. Ace lifted his head, found the gap between her leggings and her ankle socks, and gave her leg a lick.

She laughed. "That tickles, Ace."

As she was petting the dog, Marshall wandered past the door. He paused, stuck his head in the door.

"Ace isn't causing any trouble is he?"

"No, he's adorable. How old he is? He seems to spend a lot of time resting by the fire."

"Ace and I kind of found each other one day so I'm not sure how old he is. But he's healthy. Eliza and I take him out snowshoeing or cross-country skiing with us almost every day. It's just an hour—that's all the time we can spare—but Ace gets a good workout, so he enjoys his downtime."

Willa was impressed. "That's great that you and Eliza make the time for each other."

"I'd never see her otherwise. Even when you have hired staff—and Jo and Ella are great—running a B&B is more of a lifestyle than a job."

"I haven't met Jo or Ella yet."

"They're local women who do all the cleaning and the laundry. We couldn't run the place without them." He gave her a friendly nod. "Right now, though, I'm going out to shovel snow one more time. Hopefully it will be the last for a while. The sky is finally clear and there's no snow in the immediate forecast."

Once he was gone, Willa picked up her book. She'd started it on the airplane and was really getting into it. She was a few pages into Chapter Seven when Finn entered the room with a sketchbook in hand. He was wearing jeans and a gray sweater. His dark hair looked thick and soft, as if he'd just washed it.

"Mind if I join you? It looks nice and warm by the fire."

"One of the things on my list for this vacation was to sit and read by the fire. It's not something I get to do often in Phoenix."

"And does it live up to expectations?"

She could feel the warmth from the fire on her toes and legs, smell sweet hickory scent in the air and hear the occasional snap and crackle from the logs. "Oh, yes."

"I bet a cup of coffee or tea would make the experience even better. Which would you prefer?"

"Tea, thanks. Mint if they have it."

She glanced down at her book, but the words on the page held no interest for her, anymore.

As he poured hot water into mugs and selected tea bags from the canister on the sideboard, he mentioned he'd seen her and Scout at the Graff Hotel. "I got a really good shot of Scout when he was talking to Santa. I'll email it to you after I fix it up a bit."

"You were there?" She hadn't seen him. And she'd been

looking.

"I took a lot of photos of the hotel. It's a pretty neat place. I hear it was restored recently."

"Yes, by Troy Sheenan. According to Sage from the chocolate shop he spared no expense."

After he passed her the tea, Finn sat in a chair opposite hers and opened his sketchbook. Willa would have loved to see what he was working on so intently. But after a few moments of silence, she tried again to focus on her book. After fifteen minutes or so, she no longer had to try.

She was deep into the story when a snappy comeback from the heroine made her laugh.

Finn looked up. Their eyes met and Willa felt a zing of awareness pass between them.

She shifted in her seat. He was such an attractive man. There'd been lots of sexy cowboys at the Marietta Stroll today, but none of them were as appealing to her as this guy from Colorado sitting across from her.

Now was her chance to find out more about him.

"It's too bad your job requires you to be away from your family at Christmas."

"This year I actually don't mind."

Well that didn't tell her a lot. "Do you travel often with your job?"

"No. It takes a lot to get me to leave my chalet. I live on the outskirts of Boulder, in the mountains. Really beautiful and peaceful."

"That sounds wonderful." A lot like Marietta. And so different from her home in the desert.

"It is. What's your home like?"

"Scout and I live in a gated community connected to the golf course where my father works." They'd moved there at her parents' suggestion after the breakdown of her marriage. Being so close to family support when Scout was ill had been a blessing.

But lately Willa had been wondering if it might be better for her parents—as well as her and Scout—if they moved a bit farther afield. Hopefully to a younger community with kids Scout's age.

"What does your father do at the golf course?"

"He's the manager. He loves the sport, almost went pro when he was younger."

"Does your entire family golf?"

"I never took to it. But my mom has played twice a week for as long as I can remember. My older sister Thea played a lot too, before she married and moved to Boston. Now she has a one-year-old daughter and absolutely no time for the game."

"Sounds like you have a close family. Why aren't you and Scout spending Christmas with them? If you don't mind me asking."

She sort of did, because it was a touchy subject. Her parents had helped her so much over the years Scout was sick. Her sister said she understood, but Willa suspected Thea felt left out, especially when their mom hadn't been able to fly to Boston to help her after Aria was born.

But Scout had been really sick at the time. Willa was with him as much as possible. But she still had to work. And sleep. Her parents had filled in the gaps, God bless them.

"Since Scout was born, we've spent every Christmas with my parents. This year they decided to fly to Boston. My sister would have welcomed Scout and me, as well, but her house is small, so here we are, on our own adventure."

More importantly, Willa knew if she and her son had travelled to Boston, her parents wouldn't have been able to resist fussing over Scout, which wasn't what either Thea or Scout needed right now.

Spending Christmas on her own, wasn't Willa's first choice.

But it had seemed the fair thing to do. At least, thanks to Mr. Conrad's generosity, they weren't stuck at home, where being without family would have been so much harder.

"So you mentioned you're a nurse. Which hospital do you work at?"

"I've been doing private care since—" She stopped herself from saying, "since Scout got diagnosed with leukemia," took a sip of tea instead, and then reworded her answer. "While Scout was little it was easier to work as a private nurse, for older patients. Now that he's in school full-time I do want to go back to hospital work, hopefully as a neonatal nurse."

She loved helping babies, and thought her own experiences with Scout would help her be compassionate and understanding with the parents.

But here she was, talking about herself again, when she'd been hoping to find out more about him. "So where is your family this Christmas?"

He shrugged. "In Seattle. My mother and sisters all live there. I left as soon as I finished college. Not a fan of rain."

"And your father?"

He hesitated. "It's just my mom now."

"Sorry to hear that."

He glanced down, and she got the feeling that his loss was new. "Would you like to talk about him? It can help when you've suffered a loss."

His dark gray eyes sought out hers and she sensed something in her question had set him aback...and not necessarily in a bad way.

"Thank you. That's kind of you. But right now I'm still processing the loss."

"Of course. I didn't mean to pry..." She and Scout had both gone to support groups during his years of treatment and it had helped. "If you change your mind, I'm happy to listen."

"I'll remember that." He hesitated, then went on, "Feel free to tell me to mind my own business, but is Scout's father in the picture?"

"We've been apart for over two years, divorced for one.

Jeff does a lot of...traveling. I'm afraid Scout doesn't get to see much of his father anymore." Now was her chance. Before she lost her nerve, she plunged onward, "What about you? Have you ever been married?"

"Not even close."

"Oh." He sounded so definite.

"I'm afraid my personal observations of marriage have made me quite happy to be on my own."

"Since my own marriage ended in divorce, I guess I can't make an argument against your position."

"Yet something tells me you're not nearly as cynical about it as I am."

She couldn't help but smile. "That's probably true."

He smiled back, and she felt that same spark between them, an odd reaction given the subject of their conversation. Perhaps he was liking her despite himself.

But as she reached for her tea cup she noticed his eyes land on her ring, and, just like that, something shifted between them.

Quickly she retracted her hand. As she did so, she noticed him glancing at the Christmas tree by the window and the photograph of Mable's mother.

"Quite a coincidence, isn't it? That my ring looks so much like the one in that photograph?" Realizing she was playing with the band, she stopped and forced her hands flat on her thighs.

"I wonder if it is a coincidence. Didn't you say your client mentioned Marietta to you? Maybe he had a family connection here. Possibly with the Brambles?"

Gone was Finn's lighthearted tone, he sounded quite intense now.

But why would he care about her ring, or if it was connected to the Brambles? "The ring and my patient's desire to visit Marietta are two separate things. I never heard him talk about them as if they were connected."

"Can you think of another reason the rings would be virtually identical?" As he spoke, Finn leaned forward. She'd thought his eyes were gray, but the flickering light from the fire brought out flashes of silver and green. He seemed...on edge. But why?

"Maybe this ring—" she touched the band on her finger—"and the one in that photograph were purchased from the same jeweler. That would explain why they're so similar."

"Interesting idea." Finn sat back as if contemplating the possibility.

"I have to admit I don't understand why you find all of this so fascinating."

"I've never been able to resist a good mystery. Given your choice of reading material," he glanced at the book in her lap, "I figured you might feel the same."

FINN WAS SO caught up in his conversation with Willa that she caught him by surprise when she suddenly made an excuse about checking on Scout and left.

He must have pushed too hard on the ring.

Maybe her conscience had started to wear on her.

He had to admit she was a lot different than he'd expected. If he hadn't known she'd taken advantage of his father, he might actually admit to liking her. A lot.

Finn's phone pinged with the unique tone that announced messages from his mother. He decided to bite the bullet and go up to his room to give her a call. He caught her in the middle of a TV show and she asked him to hold while she put the recording on pause.

Once she was back on the line, he filled her in on the basics—no, he still didn't know why his father had left his nurse so much money, and no, Willa Fairchild didn't look like a gold digger. Then he had some questions of his own.

"Mom, how much do you know about Dad's family? Did Grandma Judith always live in Spokane?"

"She moved to Washington shortly before your father was born." His mother sounded out of breath as she spoke. Over the years her sedentary life style and penchant for chips and donuts had caught up to her. Finn wasn't sure what would motivate her to get off the couch, improve her diet and start living again.

But he knew lectures from him sure didn't help.

"What about my grandfather?"

"Well. He was never in the picture."

"Because he died young, you mean?"

"Because he and Grandma Judith never married. That

gold band Grandma wore—that was just for show. Back then unmarried mothers were stigmatized. Judith let everyone assume your grandpa was dead but think about it. Did you ever see a photograph of him when we went to visit your grandmother?"

"Well, no. I can't remember any."

"So…"

"Are you saying you don't know *anything* about him?"

"Your father never even met the man. And Judith certainly didn't speak of him."

He heard a sound, a lot like a bag of potato chips being torn open. A moment later crunching sounded in his ear.

Yup. Potato chips.

"But I do recall your grandma refusing to come with us on our family trip to Glacier National Park. She said she'd never set foot in Montana. That the state might be the fourth largest in the country, but it wasn't big enough for her. Made me wonder if the man who got her pregnant might have been from there."

Now this was progress. "Any idea what part of Montana, Mom?"

"No clue."

Of course not. And it was too late for him to ask his father.

Finn sank onto the bed, as a feeling of desolation washed over him. He'd never expected to lose his father at such a young age. If only he'd spent more time with him during the past two years.

"What's any of this got to do with that nurse who manipulated her way into your father's will? The girls are still after you to send a picture."

"She's not the way I imagined her."

"What do you mean?"

"She has a son, for one thing. He's around six." Small for his age, yet wise beyond his years. Maybe his parents' divorce, the loss of his father, had done that to him.

"So she has a kid. What does that change? She still tricked your father into leaving her fifty thousand dollars. Money that should have been divided between the four of you."

Not to mention Grandmother Judith's ring. But it would be wise to keep that fact from his mother for the time being.

"While you're at it you should find out what happened to that old sapphire ring of your grandma's. Your father stole it right out of my jewelry box when he left."

"Did you ever wear it?"

"It wasn't to my taste, but he did give it to me as a wedding gift. Eventually I was going to give it to one of the girls."

But which one? Maybe that was why Finn's father had gifted the ring to his nurse…because he hadn't wanted to play favorites. And it wasn't as if anyone in the family had ever expressed any interest or appreciation for the thing.

By the end of the call, Finn was ready to tear his hair out and sorry he'd made it in the first place.

Chapter Five

THE NEXT MORNING Finn was out of the B&B early, walking the path along the Marietta River, and calling his sister Molly. Molly's kids were early risers. He'd bet they were at the breakfast table by now.

"Hey Finn. I'm surprised to hear from you so early."

Molly sounded down. Maybe he'd caught her before her first cup of coffee.

"Not so sure I slept much, to be honest."

"Welcome to my life."

In the background he heard crying, then a little voice shouted in protest.

"Hang on." Molly was back a moment later. "They're in front of the TV now, God forgive me. So what's going on?"

"What's going on, is I'm trying not to feel like a jerk. Willa Fairchild is a single mom who nursed our father when he was ill and who is now trying to have a nice Christmas with her six-year-old son. That doesn't entitle her to the fifty thousand dollars, by a long shot. But I still feel like a jerk. Because it was her who was with him in his final days, when it should have been—"

Finn paused, blinking back tears. He'd been up most of the night, thinking of his father. Greg Conrad had been a quiet man. He'd always let his wife set the rules in the house and dominate most of the conversations. Finn wished he'd had a chance to get to know him better. Man-to-man. Now he never would.

"I feel the same way, Finn. Only it's worse for me. About a month before he died Dad called and offered to pay airfare for me to come for a visit. But the kids had colds and Charlie was really busy at work so I asked for a rain check."

Finn heard a quiet sob over the line.

"Aw, Molly, don't be too hard on yourself. If you'd known he was ill, you would have gone."

"That's what I keep trying to tell myself. But just last night I brought the Christmas decorations up from the basement and I found the old carvings of Dad's. Do you remember?"

"Yeah." Finn could hardly get the word out. Their father had been a talented woodsman and after dinner he'd often gone to his shop at the back of the garage and worked on his little creations. Every Christmas each kid would have one wooden carving in their stocking.

They hadn't made much of them back then. Finn could remember his mom talking disdainfully about "Greg and his silly little hobby," bemoaning the fact that he didn't help more around the house.

"We were such idiots, Molly. Why didn't we reach out

to him more after the divorce? Who cares if it would have made Mom angry. I can't really blame him for having an affair, anyway. Not when I remember the way she treated him."

"I'm not even sure there was an affair," Molly said softly.

"Really?" This was major news to him. "What makes you say that?

"I talked to him two days before he died."

Something else Molly hadn't told him before. "Seriously? How did he sound?"

"His voice was weak. But he told me he had a cold and, at the time I believed him."

Finn fixed his gaze on a slab of ice on the river. It wasn't moving anywhere. It would be jammed there until spring melt. "What did he say?"

"A few things. First, that he was glad us kids were there for our mother. He said he knew she was taking the divorce hard."

"That was—generous."

"I asked him if he was…in a relationship. He sort of laughed and said, is that what your mother told you? Then he said, no, he was on his own, and it was fine. He saw his golfing buddies three times a week and was enjoying a little quiet the rest of the time."

"Somehow I'm not surprised to hear that," Finn said.

"God only knows why Mom lied to us."

"She wanted to be the good guy." Finn hated to say it

about his own mother, but it was true. "She wanted our undivided loyalty."

"You're right, of course."

"All his life, Dad never put himself first, did he?"

"No. Except for the divorce. I'd like to think he had a little happiness there at the end."

"Me too."

For a long time neither of them spoke. Tears froze on Finn's eyelashes. He trained his gaze on the ice block again. Took a deep breath.

"Molly how much does Dad's family ring mean to you?"

"The sapphire? Now? Not much. Why?"

"It seems he gave it to his nurse."

"Really? It wasn't mentioned in the will."

"He gave it to her before he died. Mom doesn't know. If she did, she'd be furious. She thinks it should stay in our family."

"Of course she does. But when it was in the family, none of us ever wore it."

"That won't change the way she feels." Finn sank his head back, feeling overwhelmed by his task. He wasn't sure how he could help his family at this point. What could he tell them that would bring a sense of resolution?

"Finn, you sound awfully sad. Why don't you change your plans and come to Seattle for Christmas after all. You've met the woman, at least. It sounds like she's a nice person, who helped our dad in his last days. Maybe it doesn't matter why Dad chose to leave her all that money."

"It was never just about the money for me, Molly. And I still have questions that only this woman can answer."

SCOUT WOKE UP early, around six a.m. "Mom are you awake?"

She was now. "Mm hm. How did you sleep?"

"Okay. I like this bed."

"I like mine too. Want to come snuggle with me?"

"Can I bring a book?"

"Sure." Willa sat up and turned on the bedside lamp. The room was still dark, the sun wouldn't be up for a while.

She was glad she'd gone to bed early, even if the reason wasn't the best. She could understand why Mable Bramble was interested in a ring that looked so much like her mother's. But why did Finn seem so fascinated by it?

She was almost tempted to take it off and hide it away. But she'd promised Greg Conrad she would wear it, and think of him, and that was what she was going to do.

"Will you read this for me, Mom? My eyes are still sleepy." Scout handed her his newest Everyday Sam. There were twelve books in the series, and he owned all but the last one. After Christmas, however, he would have the entire set.

"Sure." Willa cleared her throat, made room for Scout to sit next to her, and then turned to the first page.

"Sam!" His mother called. "It's time to go to bed."

Every book in the series started the same way, with Sam's

parents making him brush his teeth, wash his face and hands and put his clothes in the laundry before they tucked him into bed. They treated him like he was a little boy who needed lots of help.

Then Sam would fall asleep and in his dreams, he would turn into a superhero and solve a very big problem. In this volume, Sam figured out who had been kidnapping dogs from the various families in his neighborhood. By midnight he had turned the guilty man over to the police and helped them return all the dogs to their proper owners.

The books always ended the same way, too. Sam woke in the morning and tried to tell his parents about his amazing adventure, but they would insist it had all been a dream. After all, he was just Everyday Sam.

Scout seemed to enjoy each story just as much, no matter how often she read it to him.

Only this time, when he closed the cover with satisfaction, he frowned. Then he pointed to the small print on the bottom of the cover. "Isn't this the guy who's staying at the B&B with us?"

Willa did a double take. "Illustrated by Finn Knightly." The name was in much smaller print than the author's. She couldn't help feeling impressed...and intrigued.

"I guess it is."

"Wow! I didn't know he drew the pictures for Everyday Sam! Do you think he drewed the pictures for the whole series?"

"You can ask him yourself at breakfast."

"Let's go now!"

"Maybe we should change out of our pajamas first?"

Scout looked down at his Spiderman top, then laughed. "Oh, I forgot."

It was nice to see her son happy, but this new development had Willa thinking. Maybe the reason Finn had been so nice to her and Scout wasn't because he was attracted to her—but because he needed photos of a little boy, like Scout, for his illustrations.

"YAY! I SMELL bacon!"

Scout raced for the breakfast table ahead of Willa, then careened to a stop when he spotted Finn standing by the window with a cup in his hands. Suddenly shy, he stared at the man with hero worship in his eyes.

They were the only three in the room so far, though fresh muffins and fruit had been placed on the table.

"Good morning." Finn finally broke the silence, looking perplexed. He patted his head. "Did I just grow horns or something?"

Slowly a smile broke out on Scout's face. "You drew the pictures for *Everyday Sam and The Dog Kidnapper!*"

Understanding illuminated Finn's features. "Yes. I did. Do you like that book, Scout?"

"Everyday Sam is my *favorite*. I have all the books except the last one." He glanced back at his mom who gave him a

She knew he was checking to make sure she hadn't forgotten to buy it for him.

As if. Scout asked for so little, she wouldn't dream of disappointing him. She only wished she knew exactly what she could do to make that promise of Santa's come true. If she could do that, then maybe she could help her son believe in Santa again, if only for a little while.

"The pictures you were taking yesterday," Scout asked. "Are they for an Everyday Sam book, too?"

"They are. But that book won't be available for almost a year."

"What's it about?"

"I'm sorry, I can't say. But it does involve snow. And a small town at Christmas."

There was certainly lots of snow in Colorado. Willa wondered why Finn hadn't gone to a closer small town than Marietta for his pictures.

"I can also tell you there's a scene where Sam goes sledding," Finn continued. "I hear there's a good toboggan hill behind the rodeo grounds. I'm going there later this morning to try and get some pictures. Maybe you and your mom want to come with me?"

Finn glanced uncertainly at Willa. "Unless you have other plans?"

"Please, Mom! Let's go sledding!" Scout said, just as Marshall emerged from the kitchen, carrying a tray.

Tobogganing had been on the list of activities Willa had hoped to do with her son. But now, suddenly, she was nervous. "How big is the hill?"

"Super-sized," Marshall said. "I guarantee you'll have a blast."

Scout's enthusiasm dimmed and he cast Willa a nervous glance.

Finn was quick to offer reassurance. "There must be some shorter runs for the younger kids?"

Marshall looked confused for a moment. Clearly to the outdoor adventurer, the idea that anyone—even a young child—would want something shorter and tamer, was alien. But after glancing from Finn, to Willa, then to Scout, he gave a small nod. "Sure there is. You have lots of options on the hill."

"In that case," Willa said. "We're in. But we do need to buy a toboggan, first."

"No need." Marshall set down a platter of bacon, another of scrambled eggs. "If you don't mind using an old-fashioned wooden toboggan, we have one in our garage."

Scout let out a cheer. "And will you take pictures of me, Finn? Will I be in an Everyday Sam book?"

"If it's okay with your mom, then yes." He shifted his gaze to Willa. "I do have release forms for you to sign."

Willa nodded. She'd gone through this routine with a few charities who had wanted to use her son's image to raise awareness for funding of research into children's cancers.

"The pictures won't end up looking like Scout," Finn added. "I'll use my computer to make them into Sam."

"But underneath, it will be me?"

Finn grinned. "Yup."

"Sweet!"

Willa listened to the exchange, impressed with the way Finn talked to Scout. Not condescendingly. But not over-his-head, either.

"Can we Mom, please? Go sledding? And let Finn take pictures of me?"

"It does sound like a fun plan. But we better eat breakfast first."

That reminded Scout of the bacon—his absolutely favorite, number one food—and he quickly took the chair he'd sat in yesterday. Eliza sat to his right, while Finn took the chair closest to the window, on Scout's other side.

Marshall poured himself a cup of coffee, then joined them.

"It's just the four of us this morning. Kris Krinkles left a note that he won't ever be joining us for breakfast. I guess he's not a morning person."

Eliza came in from the kitchen then, taking her place next to her husband. "And Aunt Mable wanted her tea and toast in the library this morning. Every now and then she gets her nose out of joint and doesn't feel sociable."

Willa met Finn's gaze and had to stifle a laugh. So yesterday Mable Bramble had been social. Who knew?

The next moment, another thought occurred to Willa and her mother-radar went on high alert. "Maybe your aunt is getting sick. Is there a bug going around?"

"I've heard a few people complaining about colds, but I don't think that's what my aunt has. My guess is in a few hours she'll be good as new."

Somewhat relieved, Willa glanced out the window at the piles of fresh snow. The snowman she and Scout had made yesterday gave her a crooked grin. He looked...different somehow.

Scout picked up on the change at the exact same time. "Hey, Mom, look! Our snowman has a hat!"

Sure enough, the snowman was now sporting a jaunty black top hat.

"I thought he was missing something," Finn said. "So I bought the hat for him yesterday. What do you think?"

"It's terrific!" Scout said.

"Just what Frosty needed," Willa had to agree, impressed that Finn would have gone to so much trouble just to make a little boy smile. Then again, maybe it was the artist in him, needing to add the perfect visual accent.

This theory was supported by Finn's next question.

"I was hoping I could get a picture of Scout pretending to put the hat on the snowman."

"Yes!" Scout pumped his arm with vigor. "I get to be Everyday Sam again!"

Finn passed Willa the platter of eggs, his eyes twinkling.

"You better eat lots. You *are* planning to tackle that tobog-gan hill yourself, aren't you?"

Willa wasn't one to back away from a challenge. "Wouldn't miss it." She helped herself, then Scout before passing the platter to Marshall.

Throughout breakfast, she studied Finn surreptitiously, a little embarrassed that yesterday she'd suspected he was attracted to her. At least now she knew the truth. And since they lived so far apart, it was probably better this way.

Chapter Six

MARIETTA'S TOBOGGAN HILL turned out to be ginormous. Willa's stomach was queasy by the time she, Scout and Finn scaled the peak. At their feet sprawled the pretty town of Marietta. She could see the twinkling lights of Main Street, the lazy curl of the river, and the grand oak and pine trees that grew along Bramble Lane.

Closer to hand were the grandstand, show rings, and holding pens where the annual rodeo happened each fall.

"Have either of you gone sledding before?" Finn asked.

"Scout hasn't. When I was a kid my family spent a Christmas in Wyoming. But we were sliding down a hill. This feels like a mountain."

"It's not though, Mom." Scout considered his mother's fear seriously. "*Those* are mountains. See?" He pointed at Copper Mountain, and the range beyond.

"Point taken."

Scout hesitated before adding, "It *is* a long way down, though."

They'd already gone on a trial run, using a short, gentle path that had been easy for Scout, but not, Finn declared, exciting enough for his photographs.

"I guarantee you're going to love sledding down from the top. There's tons of snow and nothing you could possibly hit." Finn studied the small boy for a moment. "What do you think is the worst thing that could happen to you?"

"I could fall off the toboggan," Scout replied quickly.

Without another word, Finn hopped on the toboggan and pushed off. With a whoop of joy, he was soon speeding down the hill.

And yet, a moment later, for no apparent reason, the toboggan was tipping and Finn was flying off, tumbling into the snow while the toboggan, now rider-less, careened the rest of the way down the hill.

"Finn! Are you okay?" Willa ran awkwardly through the thick snow, but she'd only managed to advance a few yards when Finn's laughing face emerged from a pile of snow.

Quickly he got to his feet, then made his point. "You don't need to be afraid of falling Scout. It's actually kind of fun."

Slowly a smile broke out on Scout's face.

"We can go down together for the first run, if you'd like."

Scout was sold. He raced down to retrieve the toboggan, then dragged it all the way up to the very top. Once more Finn climbed onto the wooden sled, then instructed Scout to sit behind and hang on tight.

"Ready?" Finn counted to three and then they were off.

Willa couldn't breathe as she watched them fly down the track, snow spewing madly on either side of them as they bounced down the hill.

Finally the trail leveled off, and eventually the toboggan eased to a stop. For a few seconds there was silence and Willa worried the experience had been overwhelming for her son.

But it seemed the excitement had merely taken away his breath, because a moment later he was whooping.

"Awesome! Let's do it again!"

Finn grinned good-naturedly as he grabbed the rope at the front end of the toboggan and began pulling it up the hill. Willa's heart tightened at the sight of the man and the boy, a little bit pleasure, a little bit pain. She knew Scout really missed his father, even though he could barely remember him.

Maybe that was part of the reason he seemed so taken with Finn.

Of course, the fact that Finn illustrated the Everyday Sam books didn't hurt.

Finn and Scout went down the hill together three more times before Scout decided he was ready to try on his own. Wanting to get some photographs, Finn positioned himself halfway down the hill. His camera with the lens attached was at least a foot long and terribly impressive looking, however Finn handled it with the casual air of a professional.

"Anytime," Finn called and a second later Scout was shooting down the hill.

"Smile!" Finn instructed as he took a flurry of photographs.

Scout did better than that. He laughed.

Over and over Scout raced down the hill and Finn surely had more photos than he could possibly need when he finally put the camera back in its case. He trudged up the hill, his gaze locked on Willa.

"Ready?"

She almost said no. But those green lights were sparkling in his gray eyes again, and something inside of her was sparkling too. Maybe he did want photos of Scout. But this man definitely liked her, too. At least a little. "I'll do it—if you come with me?"

By then he was at her side, and his gaze lingered on her face for a while longer before he said, "My pleasure."

Scout relinquished the toboggan without protest. "Yeah, Mom! You can do it. Don't be scared."

Finn got into position first, and Willa hesitated. She'd have to put her arms around him, or she'd fall off the sled. It had been a long, long time since she'd touched a man, especially one as attractive as Finn.

"I won't bite."

Embarrassed that he'd caught her hesitating, and figured out the reason, Willa made herself get on the sled. Lightly she placed her hands on his waist.

He laughed. "You're gonna fall off if you don't grab on a little tighter."

Without warning he pushed off, and she flung her arms around him, squeezing as tightly as she could. They were zooming so fast, at times actually levitating down the hill.

At first it was scary. A second later, exhilarating. When they hit a huge bump, she screamed. The next time she laughed. And then, just as the sled was beginning to slow, there was a lurch and she was falling, arms still locked around Finn, into the snow.

And suddenly they stopped.

Her cheeks prickled from the cold and she blinked away snowflakes.

What had happened?

"Um. You can let go now."

Embarrassed to realize she still had a death grip on his waist, Willa relaxed her arms. A moment later Finn jumped to his feet, then held out his hand.

Seeing his grin as he helped her to her feet, she had to smile too. *The devil.*

"You tipped us on purpose."

His grin widened. Then he pulled off a glove and with a gentle finger brushed away some snow that had been trapped under the collar of her jacket. For a moment he left his hand there, resting on the side of her neck.

It was such a little thing, but she wanted to lean into the touch, to put her arms around him again, this time with them standing face-to-face...

And then Scout came running. "Wow, you guys really

flew!"

Despite the cold air, heat flushed over Willa's face.

Had she and Finn just had a moment?

Or was it mere wishful thinking on her part?

FINN'S CAMERA SEEMED to have a mind of its own that morning. When it ought to be pointing at the snow and the mountains, and the little boy on the toboggan, he would sometimes find it focusing on Willa.

She had the sort of face that was transformed by laughter. The magic started at her eyes, making them bright and inviting, then spread to the wide, generous mouth that surely-to-God had been made for kissing.

Her happiness was infectious and natural. And if they'd been alone, Finn would have given in to the urge to kiss her many times over.

And wasn't that ironic?

He could just imagine what Molly, Keelin and Berneen—not to mention his mother—would say if he admitted he, too, was attracted to their father's nurse.

The three of them had been out on the hill for over an hour when a group of older kids arrived for some fun, and then some younger ones, too, with one or more parents in tow.

By now Finn had all the pictures he needed. He could have made an excuse and headed off on his own—but when Scout pleaded for hot chocolate, he ended up joining mother and son on their walk toward Main Street and Sage Carrigan's Copper Mountain Chocolate Shop.

Sage wasn't working this morning, but another friendly server was pleased to fill to-go mugs for them. They carried them to River Bend Park, and found a bench in the sun.

Noticing some friendly glances from others in the park, Finn realized the three of them could easily be mistaken for a family.

The thought made his gut tighten.

Finn had never pictured a wife or children as part of his future.

Having endured the sort of life his parents had shared, marriage, to him, was a terrible trap to avoid.

His sister Molly's marriage was somewhat better, but still no ad for wedded bliss. Her husband traveled a lot with his work. Molly seemed to be always alone with the rug rats and vaguely disgruntled.

Ironically his gaze was drawn to the window display of a bridal store where a beautiful white dress made a deceptive fairy-tale promise.

Romance didn't lead to happily-ever-after, but to a lifetime of bills, and crying children and honey-do chores.

Finn shifted his gaze upward to a small jewelry store above the bridal shop.

How convenient. First buy the rings, then the dress.

"J. P. & Sons, Montana Jewelers."

Finn started, surprised that Willa was reading aloud the

sign that he'd just been looking at.

"It looks so old and interesting," she said. "Nothing like the modern chain-store jewelry places you see in every mall."

Something clicked in Finn's brain as he remembered why he was here in Marietta, hanging out with this particular woman and her small, sometimes too serious son. "I wonder if the store dates back to the eighteen hundreds. It looks old enough. Maybe whoever works there might know something about your ring."

Willa was quiet for a moment, no doubt recalling that she'd been the one to spout a theory of the same jeweler designing both rings.

"I suppose it couldn't hurt to ask."

ON THEIR WAY toward the jewelry shop, they ran into Sage Carrigan, her husband Deputy O'Dell and their two children. Dawson had the baby in one arm, and was holding Sage's hand with the other. Skipping in front of them was their older daughter. Fairness made Finn acknowledge that in this particular case, marriage seemed to suit all the parties involved. Before hellos had even been exchanged, Savannah was asking Scout if he liked playing with Legos.

"I'm going to make a Santa's Village. Want to help me?"

Willa's instinctive reaction was to shake her head. But when her son pulled pleadingly on her hand, and Sage seconded her daughter's invitation with friendly insistence, she relented.

"You're sure it isn't too much trouble?"

"Savannah's been so bored since school let out and her best friend is away for the holidays," Sage explained.

"You'll be doing us the favor," Sage's husband agreed. "I can bring Scout back to the B&B in a couple hours if that works for you?"

Though Willa had only met these people a few days ago, Sage's relationship to Eliza at the Bramble House, and the fact that O'Dell was a local deputy, made the play-date an extremely low-risk proposition. Yet Finn was surprised when the super-protective Willa actually let her son leave with the young family.

By the tense lines around her mouth and eyes, though, he could tell it wasn't easy for her.

What made her so protective? Was it the responsibility of being a single mother...or something more?

"You think I'm one of those obsessively controlling mothers," Willa said, obviously picking up on his thoughts.

"Hey, I don't have kids. Who am I to judge?"

"In my experience, few people can resist judging mothers. The thing is, I'm trying to loosen up where Scout is concerned. It's just...difficult for me."

Finn was surprised to see actual pain in her eyes as she said this. "You're a good mother. Even I can tell that. You shouldn't be so hard on yourself."

When she shot him a grateful smile, he had one of those dangerous impulses again, to hold her. Kiss her.

Planting his fists firmly into his jacket pockets, Finn raised his eyes to the upper level jewelry store.

Willa nodded at the silent reminder, then followed him inside the building and to a narrow set of stairs. Each step had a unique squeak, so their procession upward was a noisy one.

Finally they emerged in front of an old wooden door with a frosted window. A small sign instructed them to press a buzzer for admittance.

Willa removed her mitten and pushed her finger on the button. An irritatingly loud buzz was followed by the sound of shuffling footsteps. Slowly, with a harsh squeak, the main door opened outward, releasing a lemon-oil scent and a small, stooped man.

The man had a bald head and watery blue eyes that seemed singularly disinterested.

"I don't carry engagement rings." He had a wavering voice that befitted his obvious age.

"We're not here to buy anything. We have this ring—it's a Montana sapphire—and we were wondering if you could tell us who made it."

On cue, Willa held out her right hand.

The older man stepped forward, peered at the ring. "My." His voice was stronger, suddenly, alert and engaged. "You'd better come in."

The shop was dimly lit, but dust-free, with antique oak display cases from another era. At the far end, an old-fashioned cash register stood at the ready—clearly debit or credit cards were not the preferred option.

"My name is Jon Paul Pendleton. Everyone calls me J. P. This business has been in our family for three generations. May I ask who you are and what brings you here?" His eyes were on the ring as he asked the question.

"I'm Willa Fairchild. My son and I live in Phoenix." Willa was quick to dispel the impression they were a couple.

"While I live in Boulder, Colorado," Finn added. "Willa and I met a few days ago. We're both staying at the Bramble House B&B."

"Ah." J. P. nodded. "Has Mable Bramble seen this ring?"

Willa glanced at Finn before answering. "Yes. She seemed to think it was identical to one her great-grandmother used to wear. Which seemed like quite the coincidence."

"We wondered if maybe the same jeweler had made several copies of the same ring," Finn added.

J.P. made a non-committal noise, then asked if he could see the ring again.

Willa slid it off her finger and passed it over.

"Beautiful," he murmured. He went behind his counter and examined the piece with a magnifying glass under a bright light, all the while making little noises of approval and mounting excitement.

Finally he returned the ring with some reluctance. "The filigree work is distinctive. I am almost certain this ring was crafted by my grandfather. And if that is the case, then it raises some very interesting questions regarding the provenance of the stone."

"It's a Montana sapphire, right?" Willa already had the ring back on her finger.

"Yes, otherwise known as corundum, which is a crystalline form of aluminum oxide. The addition of trace amounts of iron and titanium is what gives the gem its trademark blue color. The quality of this stone is remarkable. Reminiscent of the Yogo sapphires from Judith Basin County. But, different. May I ask where you obtained your ring?"

"It was a gift," Willa said a touch defensively. "From a gentleman who died recently. Greg Conrad. He told me the ring belonged to his mother."

"Do you happen to know her name, or if she was connected in any way to the Bramble family?"

"J—" Finn almost blurted out his grandmother's name, then recovered and deflected the question to Willa. "Did your patient tell you his mother's name?"

"I'm afraid not." She looked back at the jeweler. "Do you know how many of these rings your grandfather made?"

"He was very secretive about the pieces he made for the Brambles. But my father told me there had been four rings and one necklace. The stones were reputably from a small vein of sapphires the Brambles found on their stake at Copper Mountain. Up until now I never believed the story. But this stone…it does make me wonder."

Finn was intrigued. "You mean the Brambles were looking for copper and found sapphires?"

"They did, in fact, find copper. But it was all mined out in about twenty years. Marietta almost went bust when the copper was gone, but thanks to the ranchers and the founding families who decided to stay put and reinvest their money in local businesses, we managed to survive and eventually to thrive."

"What about the sapphires? Did they really find them on Copper Mountain?" Willa wondered.

"That is an unresolved question, to this day. There are some old-timers who say it was all a rumor."

Finn leaned against the counter, fixing in on the older man's cloudy blue eyes. "But you don't believe that, do you?"

"I did. Until today." The old man's voice lowered to a whisper. "If the quality of this stone is any indication, the Brambles may have uncovered a real treasure. I don't know how they managed to keep it such a closely guarded secret."

Finn noticed Willa close her hand protectively over the ring. She'd been growing progressively paler as the conversation progressed. It was left to Finn to ask the obvious questions. "If your theory is correct, then where are the other rings and the necklace? Not to mention the rest of the gems the Brambles mined from the mountain?"

J. P. shrugged. "I have no idea. But before you leave may I see the ring one more time?"

With some reluctance Willa gave it to him.

"Interesting." J.P. peered at the inside of the band for over a minute, then he passed the ring back to Willa. "Tell me. Do you see an inscription on the inside? It's very faint."

Willa put the ring under the bright light and examined it closer. "Why yes. I can hardly see it, but I think it says...May Ball. Here. You look."

She passed it to Finn, and sure enough he saw it, too. "I think it says May Bell. Not May Ball."

"That name mean anything to you?" J.P. asked.

Finn shrugged. "Afraid not."

Not until they'd left the shop did Willa tell him her theory.

Chapter Seven

WILLA SQUEEZED FINN'S arm once they'd descended the stairs to street level. "May Bell, Finn. It's an awful lot like Mable."

"Hell, yeah, you're right." Why hadn't he picked up on that? Finn blinked in the bright sunlight.

"It's starting to seem more and more likely that this ring really did belong to someone in the Bramble family once."

"How do you feel about that?"

"Confused. I just don't get why my patient would give me a ring that was a family heirloom."

"Maybe he didn't know," Finn said slowly, realizing that of course, that had to be the case. Grandma Judith couldn't have told his father the providence of the ring. Perhaps she hadn't known it herself.

But how had his father known about the Brambles and Marietta? Why had he wanted to come here? His father's mother must have said *something* to him about his father.

With unspoken accord they headed back to the B&B, Willa's hands tucked deep into the pockets of her winter-white parka. A gentle breeze played with her hair, occasionally sending strands of it into her eyes. She didn't seem to notice.

But Finn did.

He also noticed the way the sun picked up tints of copper in her hair, and very faint freckles on the bridge of her nose. Again he felt the urge to kiss her. An urge that was becoming harder and harder to resist.

When they reached the intersection of Main and Court, they turned left, following the curve of the road as it became Bramble Road.

Bramble. The name drew his thoughts from Willa, back to the mystery of the ring. Clearly the Brambles had been an important family in this town once.

So how had his grandmother come to own one of the family's precious rings? Had it been pawned by one of the Brambles and subsequently purchased by his grandmother or one of her suitors? Perhaps the mysterious man who had been Finn's grandfather?

Or was it possible that his grandmother—and therefore he, himself—was actually connected to the Brambles in some way?

The walk went by quickly as Finn pondered the possibilities. Soon they were on the sidewalk leading up to the porch. Snow sparkled on the roof of the gracious old home and the air carried the aroma of those delicious ginger cookies.

Willa paused on the first step. "It never occurred to me that this ring might be an important heirloom, or have significant value. I really do wish I'd never accepted the gift."

If she felt guilty about the ring, how did she justify accepting his father's fifty thousand dollars? It was a question that had become increasingly puzzling to Finn. The more he got to know Willa, the less she seemed like the sort of person who would manipulate an inheritance from a sick, vulnerable patient.

"I suppose you could offer to return your patient's bequest to the family," he suggested, curious to see how she'd react to the idea.

"I have thought about that," she surprised him by saying. "I'd like to find out more about the ring, if possible. If it really is a Bramble heirloom, maybe this is where it belongs, in Marietta, with the Bramble family."

THE B&B WAS quiet when Willa and Finn entered. A fire had been set in the sitting room and there was a bowl of fresh fruit and an urn of coffee on the side table.

"No dog," Finn commented. "Marshall and Eliza must be out on one of their snowshoe expeditions."

"Actually they're cross-country skiing." A woman in her late thirties came out of the back hall with an armful of folded towels. "I'm Jo, I work afternoons. Mable is napping, our runaway bride is at the Graff, and Mr. Krinkles is in his room napping. He just baked another batch of cookies. Taste delicious, but he still thinks something is missing."

Spotting the plate of fresh cookies on the sideboard, Willa couldn't resist trying one. The instant the sweet buttery goodness hit her tongue, she sighed. "You're right. These are heavenly."

"And yet, according to Mr. Krinkles, they're still missing something."

With that, Jo disappeared up the stairs.

"I'm going to grab a book," Finn said, after devouring a cookie in two bites.

"Me, too." Reading would help pass the time until Scout returned. It would also give her some alone time with Finn. Was she being foolish to want this? Willa was afraid so, and yet, she couldn't seem to stop herself from enjoying the time they spent together.

Ten minutes later they were both settled with hot mugs of coffee and a plate of cookies each. Willa had chosen an armchair with a clear view out to the road, so she'd see Scout as soon as he arrived. Finn was by the fire, his socked feet propped on a padded stool.

She read a few paragraphs of her story, but had trouble concentrating. Scout hadn't gone on many play dates with friends and he'd only met Savannah a few days ago. He was only a few blocks away. But what if they didn't get along? Or what if he started feeling homesick?

She pulled her phone from her pocket, but there were no missed messages.

Of course there weren't. She was being silly. There was nothing to worry about. She should just enjoy the rare luxury of a few quiet hours to herself.

Again she bent her attention to the words on the page. But after reading just a few more paragraphs, her thoughts were racing again. So what if Dawson was a deputy, and Sage was Eliza's cousin. A week ago she hadn't known any of these people. Why was she trusting her son with virtual strangers.

She sighed, then looked out to the quiet street. How much longer would she have to wait?

A moment later she sensed someone beside her. It was Finn, holding a Scrabble game.

"I have a feeling you're not enjoying that book. Maybe a game will help you pass the time faster."

"It's worth a try." Gratefully, she helped him set up the board. "I know I'm crazy to worry. But I just can't seem to control it."

"He's probably having a terrific time. But even if he isn't, it will be okay," Finn said.

"Are you always this calm and levelheaded?"

"Yup. Even a room full of fourth graders couldn't crack me."

"You're a teacher?"

"I was for five years, until I got so busy with my publishing contracts that I had to give it up."

"Do you ever miss it?"

"Sometimes. A night spent babysitting my niece and nephew usually cures me pretty quickly though."

"How old are they?"

"The girl is a very bossy four-year-old and the boy is a very curious two."

She smiled at the mental picture he'd created. "I bet you're their favorite babysitter." She hesitated, then decided to risk a more personal question. "You said you don't like the idea of marriage. But don't you want children of your own one day?"

His expression sobered. "Tough one. I do like kids. I'm not sure about the marriage part."

"Your parents must have been very unsuited."

"I guess they were in love at one time, but they ended up making each other miserable. I'm not sure I want to gamble on ending up just like them."

"So. Safer to stay single?"

"Dating is fun. So far it's been enough."

The smile he gave her sent a delicious tingle through her core to the tips of her fingers and toes. What fun it would be to date this man...

But what would it be like when he decided things had gone too far, the day he told her he'd had enough, the way Jeff had done?

"Divorced mothers like me don't have much time or energy for dating."

"Doesn't Scout spend *any* time with his father?"

"We don't even know where Jeff is."

"Seriously?"

"There was a postcard from Brazil three months ago.

Scout has a collection of them from all over Central and South America." But what none of the cards had was a return address where Scout could contact his father. Jeff didn't even know Scout had been declared cancer-free.

Not that he cared, apparently.

"Sounds like your ex is a little irresponsible."

"Turns out fun and carefree musicians don't make the best husbands." She averted her gaze from the display of sympathy in Finn's eyes. The situation was more complicated than she was letting on, because until Scout got sick, Jeff had been a fine husband and father. The crisis had broken him, though.

"I know I'm being a coward. But I can't deal. I'm going babe. And I don't know when I'll be back."

Those were the last words he'd spoken to her. When a year went by with nothing more, she'd hired a lawyer and he'd gone through the necessary steps to procure their divorce.

"No wonder you worry so much about Scout. Everything is always up to you. There's no partner to lighten the load."

Yes. And the cancer had made the load so much more overwhelming. There'd been countless nights when she'd longed to have someone to hold her, to talk over the decisions she'd been required to make that day, or to spell her when Scout needed her by his side all night long.

But that was over now. Why did she have to keep reminding herself of this? She'd thought she and Scout would easily slip into a happier, more carefree life once their medical ordeal was over.

It was turning out to be a process. They would get there. Eventually.

Willa tensed as a big truck slowed in front of the B&B then pulled into the parking area...but it was only Marshall, Eliza and Ace returning from their outing. Sounds of commotion traveled from the back of the house, the opening and closing of doors, footsteps, low conversation and laughter.

A minute later Eliza came into the room, her cheeks flushed attractively. "Hi you two. How are things?" Her gaze searched the room and a line of concern appeared on her forehead. "Where's Scout?"

As Willa explained about the play date, Ace padded into the room, sniffed hello to her, then Finn, before settling at his place by the fire.

"How nice for Scout that he's made a friend." Eliza poured herself a mug of tea. Perching on a second chair close to the fire, she studied the Scrabble board, then suggested a play to Willa.

"Oh, that's good. I didn't even see that."

As Willa counted up her points, Eliza said, "Sage is such a nice woman. Between you and me, she's my favorite Carrigan cousin. And it isn't just because of the chocolate."

"But the chocolate doesn't hurt," Finn teased.

Eliza smiled in acknowledgement. "When I moved to

Marietta two years ago Sage went out of her way to welcome me to the family, which wasn't easy because I was in a real funk at the time."

"You seem happy now," Willa said.

"Things turned around slowly. First I realized Aunt Mabel was in danger of losing the house, so I had the idea to turn it into a B&B. Then last Christmas I met Marshall. We were actually snowbound at a remote ski lodge over the holidays. It seemed like a disaster, but it turned out to be the best thing that could have happened to me."

Finn looked at her thoughtfully. Willa wondered if he was rethinking his negative attitude about marriage. But all he said was, "So where's Marshall now?"

"He's got an afternoon shift at the store." A little of the glow faded from Eliza's face. "He works there full time, as well as helping me here at the B&B. Occasionally he still guides wilderness trips, but not as many as he used to."

"Does he miss it?" Finn wondered.

"Oh, yes. We're always trying to figure out ways we can free up more time for him to get away. Ideally, I'd like to go with him on some of these trips. But it's just not possible for me to leave the B&B for more than a day or two."

"A job like this really ties you down," Willa commiserated.

"It's a labor of love for me. I've always been fascinated by our family history and it all comes back to this town and this house." Her gaze roved over the room fondly. "And there's

Aunt Mable to consider. She and Bramble House are almost literally entwined. If the family had to sell, can you imagine her in some sort of assisted living? Drinking out of plastic cups and using paper napkins?"

"That simply would not do." Willa smiled at the idea.

"It was difficult enough to get her to agree to turn her home into a bed and breakfast. She's had to make some compromises, but in lieu of discovering a hidden family treasure, this is the way it has to be."

Willa twirled the gemstone on her finger, wondering if they should tell Eliza about their visit to the jeweler's. She caught Finn's eyes and when he raised his eyebrows questioningly she realized he was thinking the same thing. She gave him a subtle nod of assent.

"We heard some tantalizing stories about the Brambles ourselves today," Finn opened. "Willa and I stopped in at J.P. & Sons. We met Jon Paul Pendleton and asked him to look at Willa's ring."

"Oh, my." Eliza glanced from Finn to Willa to the ring. "What did he say?"

Finn waited for Willa to tell the rest.

"Based on the filigree work on the ring, Mr. Pendleton believes his grandfather likely designed and made the ring. Not only that, he claims his grandfather made three other rings just like this one for the Brambles. And a necklace too."

Eliza's blue eyes kept growing wider as she took it all in. "All with Montana sapphires?"

"Yes. There were rumors the Brambles found a small vein of the gemstones when they were prospecting for copper. Mr. Pendleton believes they may have stripped upward of 5,000 carats from that creek bed."

"So many of the sapphire mines in Montana have been shut-in because they're just not economic," Eliza said, her eyes glowing at the idea of unfound treasure. "But I've heard there are millions and millions of carats remaining in the ground. I suppose it's possible some of them were in Copper Mountain."

"One more thing." Willa slipped off the ring and handed it to Eliza. "Mr. Pendleton found an inscription on the inside of the band. Can you read it?"

Eliza squinted, then moved to the window where there was plenty of bright light. "Oh, my gosh. This is amazing." She went to the tree and removed the same silver frame she'd shown them earlier. "May Bell is the name of my great-grandmother."

Willa had suspected as much. "Then the ring belongs in your family."

"Originally I suppose. At one time it must have been sold or given away."

"I was never a hundred percent comfortable owning such an expensive piece of jewelry. I think you, or one of your cousins, should have it."

"I can't just take something this valuable from you," Eliza countered. "And I'm afraid I can't afford to buy it from you either. Please. Continue to wear it."

Willa wasn't convinced, but when Eliza insisted again, she sighed and slipped the ring back on her finger.

"I never thought of interviewing Mr. Pendleton when I was researching my book," Eliza said. "But a lot of the things he told you I had also heard from other sources."

"You've written a family history?" Finn asked.

"Yes. The print copies were delivered last week. I'm planning to give them out as Christmas gifts this year."

"I'd like to see one. Would you mind?"

A curious request. Willa could tell Eliza thought the same thing.

"I'm afraid you won't find any new information about the sapphires or jewelry in my book. Though I interviewed dozens of locals and read all the family journals, I didn't learn more than you did from your conversation with Mr. Pendleton."

Finn shrugged. "Given that we're staying here, in the Bramble house, I'd still find it an interesting read."

"Well, in that case, sure. I was planning to put a copy in this room eventually, anyway. I'll go get one right now."

Once Eliza left the room Willa intended to ask Finn what he hoped to learn from the book, but before she had the chance, there was a knock at the front door and she dashed to open it.

There stood Dawson, with Scout and Savannah trailing behind him.

"Hi! You're back!" The nagging worry that had been stalking her the past few hours vanished at the sight of her son. As she helped Scout remove his boots, she noticed Finn putting away the Scrabble game.

"Sorry we didn't get a chance to finish our game."

Finn slotted the game back into the cupboard. "No big deal. The point was to distract you from worrying. Now that Scout's home all is good."

She paused, then smiled brightly. "Yes. All is good."

She thanked Dawson and Savannah, and was pleased when Scout did the same without prompting.

"Thanks for everything. I had a fun time."

It was only later, when she'd helped Scout strip out of his jacket and boots and they'd gone up to their room, that she realized all was not good.

Despite her best intentions, she was still riding a roller-coaster of worry and relief where her son was concerned. What would it take for her to become a 'normal' mother again?

Was such a thing even possible?

Chapter Eight

SOMETHING WAS OFF with Willa Fairchild and her son Scout.

Finn had lots of experience with the younger set and their parents from the years he'd spent as a teacher and the numerous library and school readings he did to support his book releases. Not only that, he'd hung out a fair deal with Molly and her crew, and several of his married friends had young families, too.

Finn had run into plenty of protective mothers and even a few overly cautious fathers.

None of them seemed as highly strung as Willa Fairchild.

The fact that she was divorced from Scout's deadbeat father didn't explain it all.

There had to be something else.

Could it be related to his dad? If so, Finn couldn't think what it possibly might be.

He was on his way up to his room to check email, when Eliza returned with a copy of her book proudly in hand.

"If you're still interested, you're welcome to this copy."

"Thanks, Eliza." On the cover of the hardcover book was

a photograph of the original Bramble House. Above the image was the title, "A Bramble Family History: The Marietta Years," and in smaller font below, the author was listed as Elizabeth Bramble.

"Elizabeth is my legal name. No one calls me that, but I thought it would look more impressive than Eliza."

"It's a handsome book. You must be very pleased." He flipped through the pages, noting a section of photographs at the center.

"I am. I just hope my family likes it, too. Especially my Carrigan cousins. They weren't very happy when they heard I was writing a family history. Mostly because of their mother, Beverly."

"Do I smell scandal?"

"A little," she admitted. Then she lowered her voice. "Actually, quite a bit."

BACK IN HIS room Finn sank into the upholstered armchair by the window and cracked open the book. *A Bramble Family History* proved to be a fascinating read, and he didn't stop until he'd turned the last page.

Dusky shadows had fallen over the room. Out the window the sky was a deep, indigo blue. At some point he must have reached over to turn on the lamp, but he couldn't remember actually doing it.

As Eliza had promised, there had been scandal in her book—also some tragedy. Unproven accusations of fraud had been behind Henry Bramble's decision to leave Boston and seek a new future in Montana with his bride May Bell.

They'd had three children, a son and twin girls. The girls, Pearl and Dorothy, were rumored to be "not quite right in the head" and had died unmarried, and under suspicious circumstances, when they were thirty-five years old.

This left John Bramble to carry on the family name in Montana, which he did by having two sons, one of whom died serving his country in World War One. Leaving the other son, Warren, who had married a woman named Isobel.

Together they'd had three children. Their first daughter was the very Mable who still resided in this house.

One of their sons, Charles, had a childless marriage.

Leaving again, one son, to carry on the Bramble name. Steven Bramble had married Cordelia and they'd had three children. The girl died as an infant. The next son, John, married and had four children including Eliza. The youngest child was Beverly, mother to the four Carrigan girls, including Sage.

Beverly's life had been one of heartbreak, scandal and tragedy and after reading the chapter that focused on her, Finn could understand why the Carrigan girls might have objected to the book.

There was another hint of scandal, though, of even greater interest to him, this one involving Beverly's father, Steven Bramble. In a footnote Eliza mentioned that Steven's best friend from his school years had told her that years before

Steven married his wife, he'd had an affair with a young girl who was vacationing in Marietta with her family.

They'd met at the local diner and made arrangements for several private rendezvous. When she wrote Steven several months later to tell him she was pregnant, he denied being the father. This secret had never been shared with anyone else, and the friend only told Eliza the story now because Steven and his wife were both deceased.

Without the name of the young woman, or any other witnesses, Eliza had been unable to substantiate this story, so she'd left it as an open footnote, noting the possibility that the Bramble genes lived on in whatever progeny had been produced from this encounter.

Finn closed the book and wondered. It was a farfetched theory, the only tangible clue being the sapphire ring.

But was it possible his grandmother Judith was the un-named woman who'd had the affair with Steven Bramble?

And his father, Greg Conrad, the unwanted child?

FINN HAD ANOTHER restless night, as his mind churned over his wild new theory. While it was certainly possible May Bell's ring had been sold outside of the family, it seemed to him there was at least a fifty-fifty chance that his theory was correct. But how could he prove it?

Well before sunrise, he gave up on sleep and decided to burn off some of his restless energy with a walk by the river. As he left the B&B he noticed a woman descending the stairs from the carriage house at the back of the property. It was the first time he'd seen the person renting out the rooms above the garage.

He paused to wish her good morning. "You're up early." She was gorgeous, but the way she was dressed and groomed, she seemed more suited to Manhattan than small-town Marietta.

"Oh, hi." She glanced up, obviously only noticing him at that moment. "Sorry, I have a lot on my mind. I'm Whitney Alder."

"Finn C—Knightly." He shook her hand. "I assume it's work that has you so preoccupied?"

She sighed. "Sort of. It's complicated." A glance at her watch had her frowning. "Nice to meet you—Finn."

"Likewise. And good luck," he added, because he had a feeling she needed some.

For a few moments he speculated on what sort of business would bring a woman like Whitney Alder to Marietta. Then he shrugged and headed for the river path. Only after thirty minutes of brisk walking did he remember he hadn't checked for messages since the previous evening.

As soon as he'd dug the phone out of his pocket and powered it up, a text pinged through from his sister Keelin.

FAMILY IS FINE BUT SOMETHING AWFUL JUST HAP-PENED. NEED TO TALK. PHONE ME AT ANY HOUR. PLEASE.

For the most part Keelin was a self-sufficient, reserved

person. Of all his sisters she was the last to call attention to herself, or make a mountain from a molehill. To have her reach out this way really freaked him out. He hit the call-back button right away.

She answered after the first ring, saying his name like she was grasping a life preserver. "Finn."

"Are you okay?"

"Oh, God. No. One of my clients died yesterday afternoon. He—he took his own life."

"That's terrible." Keelin worked as a genetics counselor, but he knew only the basics of her job.

"I've been up all night. Trying to figure out what I could have done differently."

"This is a tragedy. But it isn't your fault." Finn turned his eyes to the river, while, on the other end of the line, his sister started to cry. Finn remained quiet, knowing she needed the release.

Finally she was able to talk again, and for thirty minutes he listened, trying to reassure her whenever possible that she should not take any responsibility for what had happened.

He was relieved when she started to sound like herself again.

"Sorry about the meltdown. You must think I'm a basket case."

"Yup."

"Finn!" she protested, then laughed.

"You're a basket case who happens to care a great deal

about her patients. That's a good thing, Keelin. But not easy, I'm afraid."

"There are lots of difficult things about this job. I'm always working with clients who are facing wrenching, painful decisions."

"Maybe you should consider a career change."

"Perhaps. But enough about me. How about you? Things going okay in Mariette?"

"Marietta," he corrected. "And things are fine. Though I'm not sure I care so much about why Dad left his nurse all that money."

"Me either. If she helped make his last weeks easier, then I'm just grateful to her for being there."

"Are you up to hearing a long story?"

"I'd be glad for the distraction."

So he told her about the ring, about the Brambles, the visit to the jeweler's and the things he'd learned from reading about the Bramble family history, everything including his theory about his father.

Keelin interrupted many times with questions. And when he finished with the conclusion that he guessed there was no way they could ever find out the truth, she contradicted him.

"You could do a DNA test."

"What?"

"If your theory is correct, you and Eliza would be first cousins. Cousin testing isn't as conclusive as a parentage test but it's better than nothing."

"How would that work, exactly?"

"You'd need to get a kit—you can order them online. Then you and Eliza send in saliva swabs. The lab would come back with a kinship index. The higher the value of the index, the greater the likelihood the two of you are cousins."

"Interesting. Thanks Keelin. I might just do that."

But how was he going to convince Eliza to give him a sample of her saliva?

FINN HAD JUST returned from his walk and grabbed himself a cup of coffee, when Willa entered the breakfast room wearing an ivory sweater that flattered her coloring and blue jeans that made the most of her slender legs. With her long hair swept up in a messy ponytail, she looked carefree and…hot.

He lowered his gaze quickly. He'd presented himself to her under false pretenses, he had no right to feel this way. And the situation had only become more complicated after what he'd learned last night.

Safer to focus his good mornings on her son, who battered him with a series of questions about the *Everyday Sam* books that were squarely in Finn's comfort zone.

A few times he sensed Willa's puzzled gaze on him, and knew she was wondering why he was giving her the cold shoulder.

He didn't blame her. Most of the time he was with her

he forgot she was the woman who'd taken advantage of his sick father. Then, when he did remember, he felt like a jerk for not telling her who he really was. This was so not playing out the way he'd imagined it.

Finally through with breakfast, and once everyone had gone their separate ways, Finn asked Eliza if he could talk to her privately. "I finished your book last night. I thought it was a fascinating read."

Her face brightened. "Seriously? I hoped my family would like it, but I wasn't sure if it would be something other people would enjoy."

"Well, that's the thing, Eliza. I was intrigued by a footnote in your chapter about Steven Bramble."

She set down her tray of dirty dishes and gave him her full attention. "You're talking about the alleged affair Steven had before he was married?"

"Yes. And the baby…" Since his call with Keelin he'd been struggling with the right way to put his idea to Eliza. But the situation was so awkward, all he could do was plunge on and hope for the best. "This is going to sound weird, but I'm wondering if that baby might have been my father."

For a long moment Eliza stared at him. "What makes you think that?"

He'd already decided he couldn't tell her that his father had been the patient who had given Willa her ring. "It was sort of a family secret that my grandmother had my father out of wedlock. My dad never even knew his father. Then recently, right before he died, my father started talking about Marietta. I know it's a stretch. But...I hoped you might help me prove whether my hunch is right or not."

Eliza didn't look convinced. "Is that all you have to go on? Because it seems pretty tenuous to me. Do you even know if your grandmother spent time in Marietta when she was a young woman?"

"No. But once when our family was planning a trip to Yellowstone she said neither hell nor high water would ever get her to step foot in Montana again. We all assumed something painful must have happened to her, but she never told us what it was."

"Montana's the fourth biggest state in the country. That's hardly a compelling clue."

"I know." Finn wished he could tell her about the ring. But until he told Willa the truth—and he had no idea how or when he would do that—he just couldn't.

"I would dearly love to get to the bottom of that rumor about Steven Bramble," Eliza said longingly. "But this is just more speculation."

Here was his chance. "You and I could do a DNA test to find out if we're related."

"A DNA test could tell us that?"

Finn relayed the information his sister had shared over the phone. "I could order a kit today," he concluded. "We'd probably have the results back by Christmas."

"It's such a long shot. Is there any point?"

"Maybe not. But it's not as if it would hurt, either. I'm willing to cover the cost of the test."

"In that case, sure, I'll go along with it." She looked at him thoughtfully. "If by some chance we *are* related, it would make a great addition to my book."

Chapter Nine

SOMETHING STRANGE WAS going on with Finn. After several days of hanging out together, for at least a few hours each day, he suddenly withdrew. Willa wracked her brain trying to figure out what went wrong, but all she could think was that she'd read his interest in her all wrong. Tears welled at the thought. Even during breakfast he rarely spoke to her, though he cheerfully answered Scout's endless questions about Everyday Sam.

Finn spoke very little to any of the adults, actually. A few times Willa caught him staring at both Mable and Eliza with an intensity that seemed excessive and inexplicable.

Once, when he noticed her watching, his face flushed as if he felt guilty.

Clearly he had his mind on more than just illustrating his next picture book. But she had no idea what had him so captivated. It sure wasn't her. She'd obviously imagined those romantic moments between them.

Turned out the only one attracted was her.

And every day she felt the pull toward him more strongly.

She'd find herself staring at his hands, his long elegant fingers. Or at the broad expanse of his shoulders beneath the fine wool sweaters he liked to wear. Most captivating of all was the way his mouth curved so winningly when he smiled.

Something he wasn't doing as often, lately.

About a half hour after breakfast Willa would see him leave the B&B with his camera, presumably to shoot more pictures for his book.

Pictures that obviously didn't require a little boy in them.

That must have been the reason he'd befriended them those first few days. To get the photos of Scout as a stand-in for Everyday Sam. Willa was glad for her son. He was thrilled and when the new book came out he was going to be over the moon telling his schoolmates how he'd posed for the pictures in the book.

But for herself, she was crushed. Which was silly. She'd only known him a short time. His abrupt cold shoulder shouldn't matter so much.

Thankfully she had distractions. She and Sage were developing a real friendship, helped along by the fact that Savannah and Scout really seemed to enjoy playing together. A few times their play dates extended into dinner invitations that included Willa.

Being invited into Sage and Dawson's world was amazing for Willa. Her parents were kind and caring with one another. But Sage and Dawson loved to tease and flirt. There was so much laughter in their house.

Willa especially admired their approach with their children. They were both loving and responsible. But they were so relaxed, as well.

In the far distant past Willa could remember a time when she, too, had been that sort of parent. And Jeff may not have been the most practical father, but at least when he was around their home had been filled with music. He would bring his guitar into the kitchen and play while she cooked. And times when Scout was crabby, Jeff could usually make him smile by singing silly songs.

She had to try harder to be that person again. The mother she had been before the cancer. Watching Sage she began to believe it was possible.

And then, about ten days after they'd arrived in Marietta, Scout woke up with a sore throat and a running nose.

"I'm afraid you caught a cold," she told him, after checking his temperature and finding it normal. She tried to sound like this was no big deal, but inside she was panicking.

Perhaps it was just a cold now. But what if it developed into something worse…bronchitis or pneumonia? They were so far from Scout's pediatrician. Yes, he'd given her a recommendation for someone in Bozeman, but that was such a long drive away.

Maybe she should book tickets home now, before Scout got too sick to travel.

Just in case.

Willa shut herself in the bathroom and stared at her reflection. *You're crazy. Don't overreact.* But no matter what she told herself, tension seeped into every cell in her body, and a dark, impending doom pervaded the very air she breathed. It was a feeling she'd lived with for years...

She splashed water on her face, then took a deep breath and went out to take her son downstairs for breakfast.

They were the last to arrive in the sunny dining room. Mable Bramble was at her usual chair, sipping tea from her fine bone china cup. Next to her was Finn, looking incredibly appealing in a dark gray sweater the same color as his eyes. Marshall and Eliza had been waiting for them before serving the waffles and sausages they'd prepared for that morning's feast.

Scout pumped his arm. "Waffles!"

Then, abruptly, he sneezed. Willa leaned over him with a tissue. "I'm sorry," she apologized to the others. "Scout isn't feeling well today. Maybe we should have our breakfasts in our room so we don't risk infecting anyone"

"It's just a cold," Mable said. "Don't be silly."

"It's fine," Eliza added her assurance. "Two weeks ago we all came down with head colds. Scout probably picked up the same bug. I think the virus is making its rounds."

Since Scout was already pouring maple syrup on the waffle Marshall had just given him, Willa decided to give in and stay for the meal. After she'd settled into her chair, she noticed Finn looking her way. She gave him a smile, and

116

after a brief delay, he smiled back.

Conversation focused on a new dump of snow that had fallen during the night.

"Should be great skiing up in the mountains," Marshall said to Finn. "Want to rent some equipment and check it out?"

"I might just do that."

"We can head to the shop after breakfast and I'll get you outfitted. If you want something that can charge just as hard on powder days as on hard-pack I've got a great suggestion for you."

"Awesome. I'd like to see that."

Scout took in the conversation with interest. "Can we go skiing today, too, Mom?"

Willa paused for a moment, noting that Finn did not jump in to invite them to join him. Not that she wanted him to. She was definitely not ready to send her six-year-old son careening down a bona fide mountain, even if he wasn't sick. "Since you have a cold we should plan an indoor activity. Want to see a movie?"

Scout's face fell. "Nah. Can we phone Savannah? Maybe she'll go sledding with me."

Even as he spoke, his nose was running. Willa reached over with another tissue. "Sledding is not an indoor activity young man."

He sighed, then picked up his fork and resumed eating.

Willa monitored every bite he took. She was relieved

when he put away most of two waffles, a sausage and a glass of orange juice. The fact that his appetite was normal had to be a good sign. He did look a little pale, though, and his nose just wouldn't stop running.

The fifth time she reached over to him with a tissue, he scowled at her.

"Mom..."

"Stop fussing over the child," Mable said. "He has a common cold, not the black plague."

Willa flinched at the sharp comment, and Eliza was clearly not impressed either.

"Aunt Mable, please."

"Please what? Refrain from stating my opinions in my own home? I simply don't understand why today's parents must constantly dote and fuss over their children."

Mable folded her napkin and placed it beside her plate. "Excuse me. I'd like to take my tea to the library now, Eliza."

After the elderly woman made her regal exit, Eliza reached over to touch Willa's hand. "I apologize for my aunt. She can be quite...caustic."

"It's fine." Willa put on a smile hoping to smooth over the moment, even though it did hurt to have her mothering criticized so openly.

"Thank you for being so understanding." Eliza sighed, then pushed away from the table. "I'd better put together her tea tray before she gets really crabby."

"Funny how the people who don't have kids often have

the most advice on how to raise them," Marshall observed, as he, too, rose from the table and began clearing the dishes.

"Those who can't do, teach," Finn agreed.

Willa appreciated everyone's efforts to make her feel better, but at this point she just wanted to get her son back to their room. "Come on Scout, let's go brush our teeth."

"I'm not finished my waffle." Scout folded his arms across his chest and pushed out his lower lip.

At most there was one bite left on his plate. She waited, then sighed as he pushed the tiny square of waffle into a pool of syrup and left it soaking. Even when he'd been at his sickest, Scout had always been an easygoing, affable child. Willa hoped this wasn't a new stage he was entering.

Finally, after what seemed an age, Scout picked up his fork and popped the last bite into his mouth.

After Scout's reluctant thank you and good-byes, Willa led the way to the second story. On the landing her son paused in front of the door to the Red room.

"I don't believe Kris Krinkles is really staying here."

"We haven't seen him, it's true. But Eliza and Marshall say he is."

"Why doesn't he ever eat breakfast with us?"

"I don't know."

"I bet there's no one in the room. Can I peek in and check?"

"Of course not."

"I bet it isn't locked."

"That's no excuse for violating someone's privacy."

Once again Scout scowled, leaving Willa wondering what had happened to her sweet little boy. "You sure woke up on the wrong side of your bed today."

Or maybe he was feeling worse than he was letting on. She was about to check his forehead again when her phone rang. Seeing it was Sage, she answered.

"Hi Willa!"

Just the sound of Sage's cheerful voice made Willa smile.

"Savannah and I were wondering if you and Scout would like to come skating with us on Miracle Lake. We're getting a big group together. It will be a chance for Scout to meet some new friends."

"That does sound like fun. But Scout woke up with a cold and besides, neither of us knows how to skate."

At the word "skate" Scout went on alert. He grabbed Willa's free hand and gave it a tug.

"Is it a bad cold? Savannah powered through hers last week. It didn't slow her down much. There's a booth where you can rent skates. None of us are experts, we just go out to have some fun."

Oh how lovely it would be to have Sage's attitude, to not feel a cold was something to worry about. "It's a tempting offer, but just to be safe we're going to have a quiet day."

Sage told her she understood, but to call if she changed her mind. Willa could hardly hear her. Scout was still tugging on her arm and practically shouting at her.

"I want to go skating, Mom. Please. I'm not sick. It's only a cold."

Once she'd ended the call, Willa crouched to give Scout her full attention. "The way you're acting right now, I suspect you're feeling worse than you let on."

Scout suddenly went quiet. "If I'm nicer will you let me go?"

Oh Scout. "I'm sorry, honey. Not today. But I promise I will take you skating when you're feeling better."

Out went the bottom lip again. "It's not fair. You said I'd get to do everything other kids get to do once my cancer went away."

Willa caught her breath. Her son was definitely punching below the belt today. And then she heard a creak on the stairs behind her. Scout's eyes widened, and he rushed into their room, slamming the door.

Slowly Willa turned. She had a pretty good idea who Scout had seen coming up the stairs behind her. And she was right.

From the sympathetic look in his eyes, Finn had heard Scout deliver that last bombshell.

Chapter Ten

CANCER. THE WORD echoed in Finn's head as he watched Scout storm into his room. Then Willa turned to face him, her complexion pale, her eyes wide and sad.

For a few moments neither of them said a word. A lot of puzzle pieces were falling into place for him. The strange feeling he'd had that first morning, watching them make that snowman. Willa's over-protectiveness. Scout's vacillating moments of bravery and fear.

He couldn't imagine how tough it had to be for a little guy like Scout to have to deal with a serious illness like cancer. It seemed so wrong. And it must have been even harder for Willa, to be the mother and fully capable of understanding the gravity of the situation. No wonder she sometimes got so tense and worried. She'd probably spent years on the alert for the smallest change or problem with her son.

Willa's gaze turned to the door. Fearing she was going to dash off, Finn put a hand on her shoulder. "Tell me."

Her thick dark lashes gleamed with unshed tears. She expelled a long, shaky breath, then found her voice. "It's true. Scout's been…a very sick boy, for a long time. He's better now, but at times, it's hard for either of us—mostly me—to believe it's true, that the cancer really is gone."

Every worry and every question he'd had in the past six months—regarding his father's will, regarding the Brambles, regarding pretty much everything—suddenly seemed inconsequential. "What kind of cancer was it?"

"Acute lymphocytic leukemia."

"And it's gone now?"

She nodded, but there was no relief evident in her eyes. "So they say. But it can come back, so it's impossible not to worry." She glanced at the closed door to her room, then lowered her already quiet voice to almost a whisper. "Boys are at a higher risk for relapse than girls."

Instinctively Finn reached out to her, and as she let him draw her near, he rested his cheek against the cloud of her hair. "I'm sorry, Willa. Sorry you and Finn had to endure something so awful."

After a few seconds she drew in another deep breath, then pulled away. "Thanks. The hug—felt good. But I should get back to Scout."

He tried to put himself in her shoes. No doubt she had to be worrying about Scout's cold, if it truly was just another bug, or a sign the cancer could be coming back. Being alone all day probably wasn't what she or Scout needed.

"Would you and Scout like to come to the matinee this afternoon? I think there's a two o'clock showing of *It's a*

Wonderful Life."

"I thought you were going skiing?"

The prospect of chasing powder suddenly seemed unappealing. "The snow will still be there tomorrow."

She studied his face, probably trying to figure out his motives. Finn couldn't blame her. He'd been pretty unfriendly the past week or so.

"I apologize if I've been preoccupied recently. Some family stuff came up and I let myself get buried under it all."

"Anything you want to talk about?"

"It's complicated. Maybe another time."

"Then I say yes to your invitation to the movies. As long as Scout is up to it."

SCOUT WASN'T THRILLED about seeing a movie that wasn't animated and didn't have any identifiable action heroes, but after a morning of quiet games and books at the B&B he agreed to the outing. Mostly, Willa thought, because Finn was going to be there. Plus, she'd promised him popcorn and an orange soda.

Though his nose was still running, Scout had no fever or headache and his energy level and appetite were both fine. During a lunch of chicken noodle soup and grilled cheese sandwiches at the Main Street Diner, Willa gave herself a silent pep talk about keeping a positive attitude. She was going to kill herself with worry if she suspected cancer every time Scout sneezed. Worse, Scout might pick up on her anxiety and become scared himself.

They met Finn in front of the Palace Movie Theater at quarter to two.

It worried Willa, the way her pulse raced at the sight of him. But she couldn't help it. He cut a fine figure in his jeans and dark pea coat, a tartan scarf twisted casually around his neck. And his smile seemed so genuine, as if he truly was excited to see them, too.

When they were about forty feet apart, Finn lobbed a snowball that flew just over their heads, then splatted on the door to the antique shop behind them.

Scout took up the challenge, grabbed a handful of snow and retaliated. Finn caught the projectile and grinned. "You've got a good arm."

Scout looked pleased, then suddenly turned shy, ducking his head and moving close to Willa.

She thought she knew why. Putting her hands on Scout's shoulders she crouched to his level. "Are you embarrassed because he heard you say you had cancer?"

After a moment, Scout nodded.

"It's nothing to be ashamed of son. You were so strong and brave during all your treatments. I was so proud of you, and I still am."

Finn caught up to them then, and from his expression Willa could tell he'd overheard her.

"I agree with your mom, Scout. You're a brave boy. Maybe one day my writing partner and I will put out a book called *Everyday Sam Beats Cancer.* I bet lots of kids would like to read a story like that."

Scout shrugged. "Most kids don't like to talk about it."

"Why is that?"

"Mom says it makes them scared. It used to make me scared, too."

"Scout didn't want anyone on this holiday to know that he'd had leukemia. He's tired of friends and family treating him like he's…fragile." Even worse, a lot of people, even adults, had acted as if his ALL was contagious. Willa often wondered if they had any idea that their avoidance felt like rejection.

"I just want to be a normal kid."

"I can understand that." Finn squeezed his shoulder. "But the way I see it, you're better than normal Scout. Just saying."

"Cause I get to be in an Everyday Sam book?"

"For that reason and a lot more, too."

Scout's grin marked the first time he'd seemed genuinely happy all day. Willa felt incredibly grateful to Finn for handling the situation so well.

"Now are we still okay to watch the movie?" Finn asked. "Or would you rather continue on with the snowball fight?"

"Snowball fight!"

"Movie," Willa countermanded, shaking her head at Finn for opening that door.

"Movie it is, but don't worry Scout. We'll have the

snowball fight later."

"Awesome!"

Finn had already purchased their tickets, and when he heard about the promised popcorn and soda, he insisted on paying for that, as well as another popcorn and water for Willa.

They sat with Finn in the middle, and as the credits rolled, Willa felt a pang of nostalgia, remembering the times she'd watched the movie with her family, back when she was a child.

She sensed Finn's eyes on her, and when she turned to look over her son's head she saw that she was right.

"When's the last time you saw this?" he asked.

"I guess when I was fourteen. Maybe fifteen."

His eyebrows went up. "I watch it every year."

"Seriously?"

He nodded. "I'm sentimental. It's one of my many character flaws."

She laughed and shook her head at him. "Some flaw."

For the first while, Scout was absorbed with his popcorn and drink. Willa couldn't tell how much of the story he was absorbing, but when the second bell chimed and her son whispered, "That means there's a new angel, right Mom?" she knew he was taking in some of it, at least.

Forty minutes into the show, Scout needed to use the restroom.

"I'll take him," Finn offered.

When she tried to protest, he put a hand on her shoulder. "I know the script by heart. You stay and enjoy."

Willa was only too happy to sink back into her seat and do as ordered. Almost an hour later, she was still riveted when she felt Scout's head sag against her arm. He'd fallen asleep.

"It's a long movie for a little guy," Finn noted quietly.

Willa nodded, unable to speak because of the lump in her throat. George was having his crisis of faith on the bridge, and his guardian angel was trying to save him.

FINN KNEW EVERY camera angle in the movie, every line of dialogue. So it was much more interesting to watch Willa than the screen. She was totally engrossed in the story, and as she connected with the characters on the screen, he could feel himself connecting with her.

He was done with trying to resist the attraction.

He loved that she cared so much. About her son. About this movie. And clearly, at one time, about Finn's father. If he and his sisters couldn't have been with their dad in his final hours, Finn was grateful that this woman had been there.

The mystery of the ring and the Bramble family tree that had preoccupied him so much this past while, no longer seemed to matter.

All of that belonged to the past.

Whereas Willa, and her son, they belonged to the present.

And possibly, the future.

The thought hit him in about the same amount of time it took to snap a photograph. And it left him stunned. He'd never met a woman yet who made him think farther ahead than a month.

But why was it so incongruous that a man who loved *It's a Wonderful Life* the way he did, should be opposed to having a wife and a children?

The key thing, of course, was picking the *right* wife.

Scout woke up when the movie ended and the lights came on. He rubbed his eyes, "What happened? How did it end?"

"It ends with forty-three new angels," Finn told him, winking at Willa.

"Seriously? That's a lot of angels. Can we watch that movie again sometime, Mom?"

"Every Christmas, honey. It's going to be our new holiday tradition."

THAT EVENING, AFTER Scout fell asleep, Willa had a feeling Finn would be waiting for her in the sitting room, and she was right. Only he wasn't sitting in his regular chair by the fire, but on the sofa across from it. As soon as he saw her, he patted the cushion next to him.

Happily she sat next to him.

She had no idea what the family problems were that had

caused him to be so distant the past week, but today had been wonderful.

After the movie they'd gone to Bramble Park for a no-holds barred snowball fight, which Scout had loved. Then they'd had a nice dinner at the Graff Hotel where Finn had asked Scout why he liked the Everyday Sam books so much.

Her son's answer had stunned her, in a good way. "Because grown-ups don't think kids can do amazing things."

"But they can, right?" Finn had replied.

"Yup. Like I beat cancer."

That conversation kept replaying in Willa's mind. She loved the new confidence she'd heard in her son's voice. She needed to help him be proud of himself for fighting his disease, rather than feeding the image of himself as sick and weak.

"Want to tackle the Scrabble board again?" Finn asked.

Actually, she was pretty happy just sitting beside him. But she said yes and wasn't surprised to find that Finn was a ruthless competitor, not above using two letter words she'd never heard of to make double use of triple letter squares. She retaliated with a seven letter word, earning a fifty point bonus.

When the game was over and they were putting away the tiles, Finn casually asked if she was okay talking some more about Scout's illness.

The segue to a serious topic caught her by surprise, but

maybe it was a good sign that Finn didn't want to skirt the difficult subjects the way Jeff had. "Sure. Just let me run up and check on Scout."

She found her son fast asleep, his breathing calm, his temperature normal. Thank God, maybe the cold would be a mild one.

When she returned to the sitting room Finn was settled comfortably on the sofa, his arm stretched out along the back, creating a space for her to sit. All he had to do was move his hand slightly in order to tuck a strand of her hair away from her eyes.

The little touch made her nerves pop and sizzle, just like the logs ablaze in the fireplace.

Willa wished she could just focus on how pleasant it felt to be sitting here with Finn. But if their relationship was to progress, he needed to know what she and her son had been through. And she needed to know if he was the sort of man who could handle the possibility that the cancer might reoccur.

"What would you like to know?"

"How did you find out Scout had leukemia?"

"A few months after his second birthday he began crying whenever I hugged him or tried to pick him up. I found out later that this was caused by a buildup of leukemia cells near his bones and inside his joints. At the time I just figured he was achy from the flu, especially since he began running a fever too. But unlike most flus, this one didn't pass in a few days or even in a week. A few times I saw Scout curled up in bed, holding his head, and I knew he was in pain despite the doses of children's pain and fever medicine I was giving him."

Seeing Finn listening intently, she went on.

"I took him to his pediatrician and the initial blood test had her concerned. We had to go back for a bone marrow aspiration and biopsy, and when the results came back our worst fears were confirmed. Scout was diagnosed with acute lymphocytic leukemia."

Finn's hand settled on her shoulder, a warm and comforting presence.

"You must have been devastated."

"That's a pretty accurate description. I tried to be brave and strong for Scout. But inside, I was crumbling."

"And Scout's father?"

"Jeff came with me the day the pediatrician discussed the diagnosis with us. We'd left Scout with my mom, and the doctor laid it all out for us. The phases of treatment Scout would have to go through, the side effects we could expect him to suffer, and the risks he would be facing. I was the one asking questions and taking notes. Jeff just sat there like a zombie."

"Useless asshole."

Willa had to agree. "That was the last appointment Jeff

ever came to. And a month later, he was gone, period."

For a long time Willa had been angry at her husband. Not so much that he hadn't been able to support her, but that he hadn't been there for Scout.

Eventually, however, she'd had to let go of the anger. She just didn't have the energy for anything but her son, and helping him get through his treatment program.

"How did you cope on your own?"

"My parents were a huge help. I'd been a stay-at-home mom when Jeff left. Without his paycheck—he was working as a music teacher at the time—I couldn't even cover our rent. My parents helped Scout and me move into a small condo in their gated community. And Mom offered to babysit Scout so I could go back to work part-time. I couldn't commit to a regular work shift at a hospital, so I worked for private patients, mostly in the night, so my days would be free to take Scout to his appointments."

"Your husband didn't contribute financially after he left?"

"Maybe he figured his contribution was our savings account and retirement funds. Those lasted about eight months." She grimaced. "Because he had no fixed address, or job, I couldn't garnish his wages or anything."

"What about the medical expenses? Did you have insurance?"

"We'd been covered as long as Jeff was working. After

that—it got complicated. I have to say, it really sucks to be stressed about money when you're trying to help your kid survive cancer."

Chapter Eleven

A S SOON AS he asked the question about medical insurance, Finn knew why his father had left Willa that fifty thousand dollars. It hadn't been the confused action of a sick man. Nor had his father been somehow manipulated, seduced or tricked.

The bequest had been one final kind action from a man who had spent his entire life worrying more about others than he ever had about himself.

Finn felt as if his father's guardian angel was whispering in his ear, telling him that his dad had been a good man. That he'd made a difference in this world. And one of those differences was helping a single mom cope with the medical bills of her seriously ill son.

"I'm so sorry you had such a rough go of it, Willa."

"I was lucky. I had my parents. And I also had a very kind patient." She held up her right hand, the one with the sapphire.

And the next thing Finn knew she was telling him the story of his father.

"Greg Conrad was dying of pancreatic cancer himself

when I met him. I wasn't in the habit of sharing details of my personal life with my patients, but somehow he managed to worm the entire story out of me, bit by bit, during the long, sleepless nights before he died."

Finn's gut wrenched as he pictured the scene she was describing.

"He told me he appreciated how kind and patient I was, but that he could see in my eyes that I was worrying about something. So I told him my son had only recently been cured of leukemia, and that it was hard to believe he was finally better. Harder still not to worry about the possibility the cancer could come back."

"What are the chances of that happening? Do you know?"

"Our doctors are optimistic. But even if I had a ninety-five percent guarantee, it wouldn't be good enough for me."

"I can understand that."

"The night I told my patient about Scout was the night he gave me this ring." She gave it a gentle twist. "I had no idea he also called his lawyer the next day and had his will changed to leave me fifty thousand dollars. I would have tried to talk him out of it, had I known."

"But I bet the money will come in handy."

"I owe twice that amount," Willa confessed. "So, yes, it will be very handy."

Now was the time, Finn knew. He had to tell her who he was, and hope like hell she would forgive him for not telling her sooner.

He looked into her warm eyes. She was such a caring person. He hoped she would understand why he'd done what he'd done.

"Willa—"

"Hey guys, we're closing up for the night." Marshall looked in from the hallway.

Finn almost jumped. He hadn't even heard the other man's approach.

"The lamp in this room is on a timer, it'll go out at midnight," Marshall continued. "But when you're ready would you mind shutting the glass doors on the fireplace?"

"Sure, no problem." Finn checked his watch, surprised to see it was already eleven.

At the sound of his master's voice, Ace roused himself from his fireside post, took a leisurely stretch, then followed Marshall up the stairs.

Finn took a deep breath, hoping the right words would come to him. But before he'd figured out his starting phrase, Willa asked him about his career as an illustrator, what had gotten him started.

He told her about the sketchbooks he'd carried around as a kid, and how, when he and his sisters had graduated beyond picture books, into chapter books, he'd made illustrations for the stories.

Willa kept asking questions. She wanted to know about his teaching, when he was offered his first publishing deal, which of his projects had been his favorite.

While she'd already heard about the Everyday Sam books, he told her about some of the other titles he'd worked on. None were as lucrative as the Sam series, but there were a few he was especially proud of, especially the one that had earned him a Caldecott Honor.

While they talked, he kept playing with her hair, loving the texture and the way the flickering light from the fire brought out various gold and copper hues. Then suddenly, the room darkened, and the only source of light was the dying fire in front of them.

"Oh, my gosh. It's midnight," Willa said.

Only then did he recall Marshall mentioning the timer on the lamp. He gazed into Willa's eyes, wondering if she was going to say something about needing to get to sleep. But she didn't.

Then he did what he'd longed to do, almost from the moment he'd met her.

He drew her into his arms, and he kissed her.

And just like that the world collapsed and all he cared about was the caramel taste of her lips, the velvet softness of her neck, the thumping strength of her pulse, which merged with his, as he pulled her closer against his chest.

Delicious, exploratory kisses evolved and became passionate and breathless.

He vaguely knew this wasn't a good idea. It was late, but still possible for someone to walk in on them. More importantly, he hadn't told her his real name. Willa deserved…better.

But he couldn't summon the will to stop until she placed a hand on his chest, and whispered huskily in his ear. "This is nice. *Really* nice. But—I should probably check on Scout. Not to mention, get some sleep."

"That makes sense. But, damn it, I wish it didn't." He kissed the side of her neck, the lobe of her ear. Finally, he let her go. It wasn't easy.

THAT NIGHT FINN was haunted by his father in his dreams. His dad was angry, giving Finn a real talking to, something he'd rarely done in real life. Finn woke up with a pretty good idea of what had brought on the bad dreams. Today he had to come clean with Willa, and take whatever consequences that entailed.

But the second he saw Willa at the breakfast table, along with her son and Mable Bramble, his good intentions were forgotten. She looked so damn beautiful in a straw-colored sweater and dark red jeans. And the smile she gave him was transcendent.

He moved as close to her as he dared. "Good morning." He wanted to kiss her, but restrained himself, well aware that Mable's keen eyes were on them.

He tousled Scout's hair. "How are you feeling today?"

"I'm better. I slept it off."

"*Slept* young man." Mable apparently couldn't restrain

herself from correcting.

"Slepted."

Scout's attempt to make amends had Mable shaking her head in disgust. Some people were beyond help, Finn could imagine her thinking.

Eliza and Marshall emerged from the kitchen with trays of freshly baked muffins, strawberries and a puffy frittata speckled with mushrooms. Conversation centered around the delicious food, and then the weather. The blue sky and calm winds were promising.

"Going to hit the ski hill?" Marshall asked.

Finn knew the outdoorsman was disappointed that he hadn't managed to go yesterday. But before saying yes, he glanced at Willa. "What are you and the little man up to today?"

"Skating," Scout answered decisively.

Willa appeared uncertain. "I'm not sure that's a good idea."

"I'm not sniffling anymore, Mom. You said when I stopped sniffling we could go skating."

"Good point." She paused to consider before nodding. "Okay. We'll go skating. But it's going to be interesting since neither of us have ever been on skates before."

"I'd be glad to teach you," Finn volunteered.

"Oh for heaven's sake," Mable said. "In my day we didn't need lessons. We just tied the blades to our boots and got on with it."

"I'd love to have seen that," Eliza said.

Finn tried, and failed to imagine a younger Mable gliding gracefully on a pair of old-fashioned ice skates. But then, he couldn't imagine a younger Mable, period.

TWO HOURS LATER, Finn, Willa and Scout were at Miracle Lake—a frozen pond in the middle of a forest of fir and pine. At the north end two teenaged boys were feeding deadwood into a small bonfire. A shack at the east end of the lake had skates to rent and hot beverages to sell.

"I can't believe I'm finally going skating." Scout was having a hard time sitting still on the wooden bench next to the pond while Finn laced up his black hockey skates. Next to Scout was his mother. Willa had opted to rent a pair of white figure skates, mostly because she thought they were prettier.

As an artist, Finn had to appreciate the sentiment. He was just glad he'd brought along his camera.

There were no skating scenes in the upcoming Everyday Sam book, but something Scout had said to him the other day had him mulling around ideas for a new story. And a skating scene would be perfect for that book.

As soon as Finn tied the last bow, Scout was up on his feet, almost falling as he adjusted to the narrow blades.

"It may take awhile to get the hang of it," Finn warned, as he quickly laced up his own rented skates. He noticed the two teenaged boys had traded deadwood for hockey sticks and were now doing laps around the pond, easily switching from forward to backward skating, passing a puck back and forth between them.

"How about you take my hand?" Finn offered.

Scout gave him a grateful smile. Finn helped him navigate across the snow, then down to the frozen surface of the lake. As soon as his blades hit the ice Scout's eyes ballooned in his small face.

"Whoa. That's slippery."

Finn shared a smile with Willa, who was still sitting on the bench. She had her skates on, just seemed reluctant to try out the ice.

As Finn had anticipated, it took Scout awhile to feel safe enough to let go of his hand.

But then something magical happened.

Scout stopped wobbling. His strokes became more confident as he followed the instructions Finn gave him to the letter. Even the older boys seemed impressed as they watched his progress.

"You're a natural, kid," the one with the black toque said as he sped by them.

Scout grinned.

After thirty minutes he was skating laps around the pond on his own. The teenagers offered him one of their older sticks and gave him a second puck, for him to practice his shot.

At that point Finn felt it was time he got Willa out on the ice.

"I'm perfectly happy watching."

"Like I'm letting you get away with that." He took her hand and led her over the packed snow to the ice.

Her balance was a lot shakier than her son's. Finn didn't mind one bit. He told her to put her arm around him, and he did the same to her. Slowly they navigated their way around the pond, watching as the boys moved to the center, the two teenagers offering tips to Scout who seemed to catch on to their instructions almost immediately.

"Maybe he will be an NHL hockey player when he grows up," Willa said in amazement.

Finn smiled and held her tighter. At that moment, almost anything seemed possible.

As SHE CLIMBED the front steps to the B&B Willa felt as if her feet were encased in cement blocks. She was so tired! The late night, followed by hours of skating—Scout loved it so much he actually cried when she finally made him stop—had just about depleted her. Even a long lunch at the deli, followed by a mug of Sage's hot chocolate—so much better than the stuff they served at Miracle Lake—hadn't been enough to revive her.

What made her feel even more tired was the fact that Scout still didn't want to go inside.

"But it's sunny and the snow is perfect for making snowballs," he argued, following about ten feet behind her with Finn.

Finn. The brightest spot of her day, and also the cause of her exhaustion, since she'd been on such a high after their kisses that she hadn't been able to fall asleep for hours.

He'd been awesome with Scout today. And learning to skate while being held in his arms hadn't been too bad, either.

"You're still getting over your cold," Willa paused to point out. "It wouldn't hurt you to spend a few quiet hours indoors, maybe even having a nap."

"I'm not a baby. I want to stay outside and make a snow fort!"

Willa sighed. She hadn't counted on her son loving the winter climate quite this much. But before she could mount another argument against his plan, Finn jogged up next to her, placing a hand on her arm, and making her feel warm and happy all over again.

"How about I take Scout to the park for another hour or so. While you go inside and get some rest."

She searched his gray eyes for signs of fatigue. "You must be tired as well."

"A little." He squeezed her arm. "But last night was totally worth it."

To Scout's great delight, she acquiesced without any stipulations, just a simple, "Okay, you guys. Have fun. I'll be inside when you're ready to slow down for a while."

"Like *that's* going to happen," Scout said, giving Finn a high five.

Willa shook her head. Sometimes her son really was something else. She almost wished she had the energy to turn around and join them.

But. An hour of peace all to herself was just too blissful to turn down.

First thing she did was go up to her room to have a bath in the old-fashioned claw-foot tub. It was just as comfortable as it looked. Then she put on comfy leggings, layered with a T-shirt and a sweater, and a thick pair of wool socks.

Since the guys still hadn't returned, she took her novel downstairs, planning to wait for them in the sitting room.

But just as she hit the main floor landing, the doorbell sounded and Eliza came flying down the stairs behind her, dressed in another of her spectacularly tacky Christmas sweaters, this one with an applique Christmas tree, including bells that really jingled.

"Excuse me, Willa. This should be my Carrigan cousins." Eliza swept around her, dashed to the door and pulled it open.

Willa would have quietly excused herself and gone to the other room, but when she spotted Sage she paused to say hello. Sage was wearing a butterscotch-colored wool coat over a dress in a darker hue along with tall brown boots. The palette was awesome with her beautiful red hair and slightly freckled complexion.

"Hey, Willa, I was hoping I would see you here. How's Scout?"

"He's made a miraculous recovery. We were skating this morning and now he's building a snow fort with Finn Knightly."

Sage's eyebrows went up slightly as she recognized the name, but all she said was, "Great. I'm so glad he's better. Savannah will be happy too. Maybe they can get together later this week."

"Sounds like a wonderful idea." Willa was curious to see Sage's sister, who had come in behind her. She was small, fine-boned with exquisite features, dark hair and captivating blue eyes.

"You've already met Sage," Eliza said, "but I don't think you've met her sister Callan. Callan and her husband Court McAlister live on the Circle C Ranch farther down in the valley."

Callan was wearing jeans and a plain gray sweater, clothing that fit her perfectly and emphasized her petite figure.

A girl as pretty as Callan, Willa figured, didn't need much in the way of adornment to look good.

"Hey, Willa."

Callan stuck out her hand and when Willa shook it, she was amazed at the strength of her grip and the hardness of her calluses.

"Aunt Mable's waiting for us in the library," Eliza said. "Please excuse us, Willa."

"Why doesn't Willa join us?" Sage suggested. Quietly she added, "Not that tea with Aunt Mable is such a treat for you.

But the rest of us would love your company."

Willa had been looking forward to her book...and maybe a catnap. But Eliza pounced on the idea. "Yes, please join us, Willa."

"Well... I was planning to read for a bit."

Callan shook her. "You're coming Willa. Even if we have to drag you in there."

Chapter Twelve

THE STAGE WAS perfectly set for an English afternoon tea in the library. Aunt Mable sat in the best chair by the window, dressed in a high-necked lace blouse, a string of pearls and a flowing gray skirt.

She accepted kisses from her great nieces with perfect politeness. "Good afternoon, Sage." Then, with slightly less approval in her tone. "Callan, dear, so good of you to come."

"We've invited Willa to join us," Eliza said. "Isn't that fun?"

Aunt Mable's eyebrows rose at the word "fun," but she offered no comment, other than, "Interesting footwear. Your socks look very…comfortable."

"Don't mind her," mouthed Sage from a vantage point behind her aunt.

Aunt Mable assigned them chairs around a linen-covered, circular table that had been set with exquisite china for four.

Eliza excused herself and came back with a tray containing an extra place setting for Willa, as well as a silver teapot, creamer, sugar bowl and lemon slices.

A three tiered plate stand containing tiny, crustless sandwiches on the bottom layer, miniatures quiches on the second, and lemon-flecked pound cake slices on the top, had already been placed at the center of the table.

It was all quite grand, like tea at the Ritz, Willa thought, as Mable did the pouring with an arm that was impressively steady for a woman in her eighties. At least, Willa assumed Mable was in her eighties. She certainly wasn't about to ask. Now or ever.

In grande dame fashion, Mable controlled the conversation, asking about the welfare of her nieces' husbands, then about Sage's children. Once those questions had been perfunctorily answered, she turned to Callan.

"And the ranch, dear. Are you still spending your days outside like a common cowhand? Or has that sensible husband of yours convinced you your duties lie elsewhere?"

"Court values his life too much to ever suggest I belong anywhere but where I want to be. Which is generally either riding a horse, or looking after one."

Mable shook her head, sadly. "Your dear mother would be so appalled. You're nothing like her."

"Actually Callan—and Dani—look a lot like our mother," Sage said, injecting a note of cheerfulness into the conversation. "But Aunt Mable's right about one thing. Mom intensely disliked living on a ranch."

Sage had told Willa a little about her parents, so she knew Beverly Bramble had been killed in a ranching accident when Sage was a young teenager, and that their father, Hawksley, had died just last year.

"Please everyone, help yourself to the food," Eliza encouraged, looking like she couldn't wait for this occasion to be over.

As Willa reached for one of the quiches, Callan let out a quiet gasp.

"Oh, my gosh. Where did you get that ring?"

Callan was talking about the sapphire. Of course. Willa wondered why she hadn't put the darn thing in the bottom of her suitcase. She was so tired of all the attention it was attracting.

Before she could explain about the ring and all she and Finn had learned from the local jeweler, Aunt Mable said, "I'm surprised you noticed, Callan. It's just like the one my great grandmother—May Bell, for whom I'm named—is wearing in the portrait Eliza has hanging on our tree."

"Is it? It's also exactly like a ring of Mom's Dad gave me after she died."

"Really?" Eliza's eyes sharpened. "But when I was doing my family history research, I asked about heirlooms. You and your sisters told me there were none."

"I didn't know the ring was an heirloom. Honestly, I've never worn it. I'm not much for jewelry." Callan held out her hands which were adorned with only one simple gold wedding band. "Court tried to buy me a rock when we got engaged. I told him I'd rather have a new saddle."

"Well, that explains where two of the rings are," Willa noted.

"Two?" Aunt Mable asked. "You mean there are more?"

Willa glanced at Eliza, waiting for her nod, before she explained about taking her ring to be appraised by local jeweler, J. P. Pendleton. "He's almost certain this ring was made by his grandfather for Henry Bramble. Apparently there were four rings made. Plus a necklace."

Willa removed her ring and showed them the faint inscription. "This one says *May Bell* if you hold it under a good light."

"And—how did you come to own this ring?" Callan asked.

Willa sighed, but before she could recount the story, Eliza stepped in on her behalf, telling them about her patient and his odd, but generous gift.

"At the time I didn't realize how valuable this ring was. Or that it was a family heirloom."

Callan shrugged. "Maybe the ring was pawned at some point."

"That's probably what happened," Sage agreed. "We certainly don't want to give you the impression that we resent you owning that ring, Willa." She turned to her sister. "Is there an inscription on your ring?"

"I don't know. I've never looked."

"Well, would you?" Eliza said. "This is precisely the sort of stuff that should have been in my family history."

"I'm afraid you published your book too soon dear." Mable set her tea cup precisely on its saucer. "It seems there are still a few secrets hiding in this family tree of ours."

FINN GOT A kick out of spending time with Scout. The kid really was something else. Besides being naturally athletic, with boundless energy, he also had a sensitive, mature side that surfaced regularly and never failed to impress the hell out of Finn when it did.

Like when Scout came to him asking for his help in making a Christmas present for his mom. When Scout told him his idea, Finn knew Willa would love it.

For about a week he and Scout made a pretense of going outside for snowball fights every afternoon. In actual fact they would walk out the front door, only to slip in the back, where Eliza had permitted Finn to set up his art supplies on the breakfast table.

When he wasn't helping Scout with his project, he was looking for ways to spend time with his mother. Finn had a good idea what was happening to him. He was falling in love.

Maybe it was his fear of turning into his father, or maybe he'd just never met the right girl before, but this was a first for him. And the rush of endorphins was doing crazy things to his head.

It certainly impaired his good judgment when it came to telling Willa about his father. It seemed every time he found the perfect opening they were either interrupted, or Willa changed the subject before he could find the right words.

After a while, the urge to come clean, like any unwelcome task, became easier and easier to push aside.

It almost seemed like it no longer mattered. His feelings for Willa were becoming so all-encompassing that all he cared about was spending time with her and her son. In fact, he was so distracted that when the call came from UPS about a letter he needed to pick up, he put the task off for over a week, even though he knew this had to be the results of his and Eliza's DNA testing.

Even when he did finally pick it up, he didn't bother to open it. He told himself it was because he no longer cared whether he was related to the Brambles anymore. Even the prospect of secret treasure no longer seemed tantalizing.

The real reason he was afraid to open the letter, however, was out of fear that real life might be on a collision course with his newfound love. If it came to facing the truth about his father, the Brambles and himself, or spending time with Willa, well, he chose the latter.

The last ten days leading up to Christmas were filled with fun family activities with Willa and Scout. They went skating almost every day, occasionally joined by Sage's daughter Savannah and some of her friends. Scout's skill developed with exponential speed. It was exhilarating to watch him master skating backward after only a week on blades.

After chaotic, action packed days, Finn looked forward to a quiet hour or two alone with Willa after Scout fell asleep. They often began with a ritual Scrabble game, followed by quiet conversation and passionate, if frustrated, kisses.

He longed to make proper love with Willa, but finding the right moment and place was tricky. He'd checked the lock on his door, just in case, and had discovered it did work.

What he needed next was the right opportunity.

Five days before Christmas, Sage's mother-in-law, Patricia Anderson, an uber-groomed woman with big hair, fake nails and painted-on eyebrows, checked into the second suite on the third floor of the B&B along with a man about a decade younger than her, whom she introduced as Mike, her fiancé.

Via Willa, Finn learned that Patricia had been married about six times and had dragged Dawson all over the country when he was growing up. Relations between mother and son had gone through a fair amount of ups and downs, but she had come to spend Christmas with him and his family, hoping especially to bond with her brand new grandson.

Judging by the mountain of packages she had Mike carry up to their room, some of that bonding would take place by way of numerous Christmas gifts.

"Neither Sage nor Dawson are thrilled she showed up," Willa confided. "But what can they do? It's Christmas."

Hearing her say that, Finn was reminded of his own family and the fact that he hadn't heard from them for a few weeks. He'd sent a message to his mom and sisters explaining about Scout's cancer and Willa's medical bills. He'd told them that the matter was closed. As far as he was concerned, Willa had more than deserved everything their father gave them.

He hoped they agreed.

But they'd been suspiciously quiet since then. He'd only received one text and that had been from Keelin, quietly informing him she was thinking of quitting her job.

Immediately he'd tried phoning her back, but she hadn't answered then, or any of the other times he tried.

He wasn't opposed to her quitting, if that was what she wanted. He just hoped she wasn't still carrying a load of guilt about the patient who had committed suicide.

As for his work, it seemed every time he opened his laptop or his sketchbook, something happened to distract him.

Usually, it involved Willa.

He was desperate to spend time with her, but suddenly there were people coming and going at all hours. The addition of Patricia and Mike changed the dynamics at the breakfast table, and also in the sitting room in the evening. Usually Patricia and Mike would have dinner with Sage and Dawson, ending up back at the B&B around nine—the time he and Willa had become accustomed to spending alone.

"I wish I could whisk you and Scout to my chalet in Boulder," Finn told Willa one night, when they were saying goodnight in front of their respective doors.

For a moment, she almost looked tempted.

"But we're prepaid at the B&B. And Scout is so happy here."

It was true, Scout was no longer the pale, quiet boy he'd been those first few days in Marietta. His color was better, he seemed stronger and even looked taller. All the fresh air and activity was bringing him back to life.

"Besides," Willa continued, "didn't you come here to work? I'm afraid we've been a distraction for you."

Finn held out his arms. "Distract me some more, why don't you?"

"REMEMBER WHEN I took you to visit Santa Claus?" Willa couldn't believe it was the night before Christmas Eve already. This holiday was flying by much too quickly.

"You mean at that big, fancy hotel?" Scout had just finished his shower, and was now standing patiently, wrapped in a towel, while she used a second one to dry his hair.

"Yes." So much had happened since that day. Most of it wonderful. Not only was Scout reveling in his newfound health and all the outdoor activities in Marietta, but she was beginning to believe she'd found true love with Finn.

After a rough beginning, when she hadn't been sure if he really liked her, or just wanted to use her son for his illustrations, they were progressing into a love affair that felt like something from the movies. Not only did she adore being with Finn, but she admired him as an artist and as a man. So far their lovemaking had only extended to kisses, but she had no doubt that when they did come together, it would be fabulous.

But when would that be? Finn had let out some broad hints that he wanted her and Scout to visit him in Boulder for New Year's Eve. Willa was tempted to take him up on that.

But first she wanted to make sure Scout's Christmas was wonderful. Plans for tomorrow and Christmas Day were shaping up perfectly. Her only worry was whether Scout would be disappointed if Santa didn't deliver on the vague promise he'd made on that day at the Graff Hotel.

"I remember." Scout wriggled out from under the towel to pull on his pajama bottoms.

"What was it Santa said to you, again? Something about adventures?" She passed him the top to his PJs, helping at the part where his head always got stuck.

"He said was I a boy who liked adventures, and I said yes."

"Anything else?"

"He said was I a boy who liked helping people."

"And you said yes to that, too?"

Scout nodded. "And then he said he was going to make sure this is a Christmas I'll never forget."

Willa took the brush and made quick work of smoothing out her son's damp hair. "So—what do you think is going to happen?"

Scout gave her a curious look.

"Do you think you're going to have some sort of adventure on Christmas and...help someone, somehow?" She felt lame asking the question and she could tell Scout agreed.

"Mom, Santa isn't real. He's just a guy dressed up in a suit."

Willa knew she ought to be relieved her son didn't have unrealistic hopes that would only be dashed. Yet she couldn't help but wish he'd been able to hang onto the magic just a little bit longer.

FINN HAD NEVER spent a more action-packed December twenty-fourth. The morning began with an announcement from Eliza at breakfast.

"Our runaway bride is getting married to Mitch Holden tonight. They're having a candlelight service at six p.m. and Santa will be giving away the bride. Emma says you're all invited."

"How scandalous," Mable decreed. "Wasn't it just a month ago that Scottish girl was all set to marry some other fellow?"

"Best way to get over a broken heart is to find a new love." Patricia patted Mike's hand possessively.

"It was love at first sight for Mitch," Eliza said. "He's a wonderful man and I'm sure the two of them will be very happy."

"I had a call from Sage this morning," Willa said. "She's going to be handing out chocolates at the wedding."

"Awesome! Can we go, Mom?"

"Yes. And afterward, Sage has invited us to join their family for a chocolate fondue and gift exchange."

"Finn, too?"

"Yup," Finn was happy to confirm. "I'll be there."

"Cool." Scout took a drink of orange juice, then frowned. "But we still have time to go skating, right?"

"We can go skating after lunch," Willa promised. "As long as we're home by four to get ready for the wedding."

"Why can't we skate in the morning, too?"

Finn shook his head ruefully, "I see we've created a monster."

Willa smiled at him, then answered her son. "Because I don't want you to be exhausted tonight. Besides, we need to pick up a few extra Christmas gifts for the party at Sage's."

"You don't mean we're going *shopping*?" The way Scout said the word, it sounded like torture.

"Don't you want to pick out a gift for Savannah and her little brother?"

"I guess…"

"It's better to give than receive," Mable commented. "Although children these days already own far too many toys if you ask me."

Finn wondered how many of them around the table had to bite their tongues from pointing out that, actually, no one *had* asked her. Judging from the expressions on Eliza's and Marshall's face, at least three, counting him.

"What about you, Miss Brambles," he asked. "What are you hoping for this Christmas?"

The question caught Mable off guard, but she soon recovered and replied with her usual self-possession. "In my experience, it never matters what one hopes for. Scented soaps, books and chocolates are the *de rigueur* gifts once you reach a certain age."

Finn made a mental addition to his Christmas shopping list. He was going to have a very busy morning.

AT FOUR O'CLOCK that afternoon, Finn was relaxing by the fire in the sitting room with a cup of tea and his sketchbook. He was doodling when Kris Krinkles, hair and beard damp, dressed in a pair of gray sweats, came downstairs. Finn did a double take, then sat upright. This was the first time he'd actually encountered the gentleman Eliza and Marshall kept insisting was staying in the Red room.

"Good afternoon, Finn." Kris surveyed the room, gaze stopping at the sideboard. "Ah! Coffee! Just what I need. It's going to be a long night."

"I guess so," Finn agreed, amused by the man and how well he acted his role, even when off-duty.

"That fire looks cozy. Mind if I join you?"

"Please do."

Kris sank his extra-large sized body into the sofa and gave

a satisfied sigh. "Oh yes, this is perfect." He glanced at the sketchbook. "You're a talented man. I must say the Everyday Sam books are one of my most popular items."

Finn grinned. "Glad to hear it."

"I know the latest book is on Scout Fairchild's list. But I'm a bit concerned about that boy. He's very young not to believe in Santa Claus."

Finn grew serious. "He's had to grow up fast in many ways."

"Yes. That leukemia was a terrible business."

"I thought I was the only one who knew—" Finn shook his head. "Never mind. I suppose you have your sources."

"Indeed I do. I also have an idea for how we can make that young man's Christmas extraordinary this year. But I'm going to need your help."

"How so?"

When Kris explained what he needed, Finn shook his head. "Scout's mother is very protective."

"But if anyone can convince her, you can."

"Maybe." He wasn't so sure anyone on earth had that much power.

"You'll find a way." Kris finished his coffee with a satisfied "ah."

"I'll try."

"Good. I'd better get upstairs now. It takes a while for me to get dressed, especially on Christmas Eve. Every detail has to be just so."

Before leaving the room Kris planted his hand on Finn's shoulder and glanced down at his sketchbook.

Finn had been working on a drawing of Willa, the way she'd looked that morning when he'd stolen a kiss under the mistletoe at the gift shop.

"Lovely woman," Kris said. "After all she's been through, I'd sure hate to see her get hurt again."

Finn swallowed hard. "What makes you say that?"

Kris didn't answer. But he looked at Finn like he could see straight through him.

Chapter Thirteen

WILLA WAS RELIEVED when Scout fell asleep shortly after they returned to their room at the B&B. He'd been going nonstop all day and it was going to be a late night, too. While he got some much needed rest, she used the time to wrap the presents they'd purchased that morning.

Then it was time to get dressed for the evening. She put on an ivory-colored silk blouse and a long, black skirt that made her feel very elegant, especially once she put her hair up and added sparkling drop earrings.

When Scout woke up he was a little grouchy, but after eating the sandwich and bowl of soup Willa had snagged from the kitchen, he perked up a little.

"When you've finished your milk would you please get dressed, son?" She indicated the button-up shirt, nice pants and sweater she'd set out for him.

"Why do we have to dress so fancy?"

"Because we're going to church. And a wedding."

He perked up a little, no doubt remembering the promised chocolates Sage was going to be handing out.

Willa put the gifts she'd purchased for Sage, Dawson,

Savannah and Braden into a big shopping bag. "Ready to go?" Finn had texted her ten minutes earlier saying he would wait for them downstairs.

On the landing Scout paused by the door to the Red room. "Do you think Kris Krinkles is in there?"

"I bet he's at the church already."

Scout galloped down the stairs, then skidded to a stop when he encountered Eliza, carrying a platter of cookies still warm from the oven.

"Santa made one final batch this afternoon," Eliza said. "I believe these are the best yet. He made me promise that you would eat one of these tonight."

Scout looked at his mother, and Willa nodded. She'd already decided that for the next two days she wouldn't worry about the amount of sugar her son consumed.

After his first bite, Scout said, "Wow! Can I have another?"

"You haven't even finished that one." Her son was so hyped up, Willa was worried he would end up crashing before the evening was over. "Besides we have to get going. I don't want to be late for the wedding."

Finn appeared then, already in his jacket and carrying their coats. His warm smile felt like it was meant for her alone.

"Looks like you're ready to head out the door," Eliza said. "Marshall and I will meet you at the church."

"Aunt Mable, too?" Willa asked.

"Heavens no. We're having a late dinner together at eight, once 'all the fuss,' as she puts it, is over."

Outside it seemed the whole of Bramble Lane was lit up. Twinkling lights guided them as they walked to the church off Court Street. Willa realized she was growing used to the cold, winter air. In fact, she was starting to like it.

Part way there, Finn took her hand, and they fell into step together with Scout scampering ahead, fueled by his nap, his dinner and the sugary cookie.

The chorus from her favorite Christmas carol popped into her head. *Tidings of comfort and joy.* Those words described perfectly how she felt right now, a delicious combination of feeling safe and cared for, as well as incredibly happy.

There was an excellent turnout at the church, and the candlelit service was beautiful.

As she watched the bride and groom exchange their vows, Willa said a prayer for them and another for Greg Conrad. She wished he could know how much he'd done for her.

The ring and the money were the least of it. If he hadn't booked them into the B&B she never would have come to Marietta. This town was far removed from her and Scout's regular life, yet so many of the people and their traditions had touched her heart. Not the least of whom was Finn.

She caught him looking at her frequently throughout the service. The one and only time they'd discussed marriage he'd been vehemently opposed to it. She was pretty sure his feelings had undergone a dramatic shift since then, though. He seemed genuinely moved as the couple exchanged their vows.

Was he imagining the two of them getting married one day?

She certainly was.

Her feelings for him were growing stronger and stronger with each day. Tonight she planned to tell him she and Scout would be happy to accept his invitation to spend New Year's Eve with him in Boulder. She was excited to see Finn's home and learn as much as she could about the man she was falling in love with.

When the service was over, they filed out of the church. Scout was overjoyed when Sage gave him, not just one, but two of her delicious truffles.

"That was one of the nicest weddings I've ever been to," Finn commented.

"The candlelit service was lovely," Willa agreed. "And the bride and groom looked over the moon with happiness."

"I liked when Santa walked down the aisle," Scout said. "He gave a special wink, just for me."

WILLA HAD EATEN modestly all day, saving room for Sage's chocolate fondue. There were eight of them seated around Sage and Dawson's dining room table, including Patricia and Mike. The baby, of course, was too young to participate, so

Dawson held him on his knee so he could keep an eye on the proceedings.

The aroma of melted chocolate was intoxicating. Every person at the table was given their own small pot of it, as well as a generous portion of cut-up apples, bananas, strawberries and shortbread cookies for dunking.

"Merry Christmas everyone," Sage announced. "Please dig in and let me know if you'd like more. There's never a shortage of chocolate in this house."

Willa stabbed a strawberry with her fork. Then dipped. The velvety combination of dark and milk varieties of chocolate had been heated to the perfect temperature so it clung in a thick layer to the fruit.

She popped the whole thing into her mouth. Then sighed. Sublime. She chewed slowly, savoring the experience, not even realizing she'd closed her eyes until she opened them—and saw Finn watching her with a lazy, sexy smile.

"Aren't you going to take a taste?" she asked.

"I'd love to," he murmured. "But this is a family event."

She could feel her cheeks burning and not from the large fire burning in the adjoining family room. Finn was making his interest in her very obvious tonight. And she loved it. After the ceremony, he'd held her hand as they walked back to Bramble Road. Sage and Dawson's home was several blocks from the B&B, a modest, but charming two-story.

"How is it you ended up living so close to your Aunt Eliza?" Willa asked.

"It was just a coincidence. I'd been in love with this house for years," Sage said. "But I had to marry Dawson to get it."

"I was willing to get her using whatever means necessary." Dawson went along with the joke. "Even if it meant buying her dream home from under her and using it as a bribe."

"I just hope you don't feel too tied down, son." Patricia was spending more time sipping her wine than enjoying the fondue. Perhaps she was watching her admittedly very trim figure.

"Why would you say that?" Dawson sounded annoyed.

"Not that long ago you were a carefree cowboy on the rodeo circuit. Now you've got a demanding full-time job as deputy, a house, a wife, and a brand new baby. That's a lot of change for just two years."

"I worked hard to get these things, Mom. I was sick and tired of the rodeo life. Independence is a fine thing. But having people in your life who love you and need you is a hell of a lot better."

Willa glanced at Finn, and found him looking at her, too.

"From where I sit," Finn said, "Dawson is a lucky man."

Sage gave him a grateful smile, but Savannah was bored with the serious turn in the conversation. "When are we going to open presents?"

"Have you had enough chocolate?" Sage countered.

"No!" Savannah dipped a chunk of banana into the fondue, gobbled it down, then smiled. "Okay. Now I have."

They all moved to the family room, where dozens of colorfully wrapped gifts were piled under a Scotch pine tree bedazzled with lights, ornaments and garland. The room was warm thanks to the wood-burning fire, and Christmas carols played softly in the background, only rarely heard above the buzz of conversation.

The idea was that everyone was to open one gift, and save the rest for tomorrow. The gifts were all fun, nothing extravagant. Both Savannah and Scout received small Lego sets from Jurassic World, which they happily assembled and began to play with.

Willa was more than happy with her signature Copper Mountain Chocolate mug, filled with a bag of hot cocoa mix. The cocoa wouldn't last long, but the mug would forever be a reminder of the wonderful friends she'd made in Marietta.

"I wish you guys didn't have to leave after Christmas," Sage confessed when they were saying good-bye a few minutes before ten. Patricia and Mike were still in the family room. Since they wanted to watch the grandchildren open their stockings and gifts in the morning, they were sleeping over on the pull-out couch.

"I've grown to love this town," Willa confessed.

"Me too!" Scout added. "Can we move here, Mom?"

Because of his prolonged illness and all the school he'd

missed, Scout didn't have many friends in Phoenix. With the added bonus of snow and ice, Willa wasn't surprised to hear his request.

"According to the doctor who lives down the street from us, the hospital is currently looking to hire at least one nurse," Sage said. "And yes, I confess, I did ask, on the outside chance you might be interested."

"Wow." Willa felt more than a little overwhelmed.

"You, too, Finn," Sage added. "With your job you can work anywhere, right?"

"That's true. As long as I'm near a ski hill, I'm happy."

Willa shot him a questioning glance. Was he implying that he, too, would be willing to consider a move to Marietta? They had so much to discuss.

But right now, she needed to get her son home to bed. He was so tired he was leaning against her the way he had as a toddler when he wanted her to carry him.

Finn noticed, and once they were outside he scooped Scout up onto his shoulders. It was only a short walk home, but the cold made Willa's cheeks tingle. She looked up at the sky, but couldn't see any stars.

"I wonder if it's going to snow."

"I hope so," Scout mumbled sleepily. "I love snow."

At the B&B Finn carried her son up the stairs, delivering him straight to his little bed. He was practically asleep so Willa decided, just this once they would forgo brushing his teeth. Quickly she helped him change into his Christmas pajamas—dark green with a pattern of miniature dancing reindeer.

By the time she drew his covers to his chin, he was fast asleep. "Merry Christmas my darling boy." She kissed his forehead, then looked for Finn. He was sitting on a chair by the door, waiting for her.

As she moved toward him, he rose and drew her into his arms. Without a word, he kissed her.

So much need and desire had been building up between them, the kiss couldn't possibly release it all. But being in his arms, feeling his lips on hers, was definitely a good start.

When he asked if she would come to his room, she nodded.

Until that moment, it hadn't felt right. But it did now.

Quietly they left Scout, sleeping soundly on his rollaway bed. In the hallway, Finn paused. "I need to ask you something first."

Now that they'd finally made the decision to sleep together, Willa was impatient. "What?"

"I had a talk with Kris Krinkles tonight. He wants your permission to take Scout on an outing later tonight."

"Tonight?" she repeated, thinking she couldn't be hearing correctly.

"Yes. He wants to take Scout on an adventure. He has a dog sled lined up to deliver presents to the sick children at the local hospital."

Willa stared at him, stunned. "Why can't they do this in

the morning?"

"Because the children have to get the presents before they wake up."

"But…" She blinked several times, wondering if she'd had too many glasses of wine tonight. "But Scout's so tired. He needs a good night's sleep. Besides, do any of us really know this Kris Krinkles?"

"I had a feeling you'd say that. So I stopped by the Graff today and asked. They told me they did a complete background check of the guy before they hired him for the holiday season. He came with glowing recommendations from many sources. And then I checked with Dawson. He's going to be keeping an eye on the proceedings, too."

"What about the dog sled? That doesn't sound safe."

"Snowy Owl Dog Sled Tours is providing the team. They're very reputable."

Willa covered her face with her hands. This was outrageous. How could anyone expect her to allow her six-year-old son to go out in the middle of the night, during a cold Montana winter, to deliver toys from a sled pulled by a team of dogs and driven by a total stranger with Santa delusions?

"It's like an Everyday Sam book," Finn explained. "You put him to bed like he's just an ordinary boy, and then he has an amazing adventure, and in the morning—"

"—he goes back to being a regular little boy." As she said this, Willa realized, despite her misgivings, there was no way she could say no. If Kris Krinkles pulled this off, Scout would be the happiest boy in the world tomorrow morning.

"You're sure he'll be safe?"

"I am."

"And Dawson really will be watching out for them the entire time?"

"Yes."

She took in a deep breath. "Well. Okay. I give my permission."

Finn looked relieved. "I'm glad. I think this is going to be just what Scout needs." He took a red ribbon from his pocket and tied it to the door knob of the Blue room.

"What's that?"

"This will let Kris know you're on board with the idea."

She tried to swallow but her mouth was too dry. "I hope I'm doing the right thing. I know for sure I won't sleep a wink until this whole thing is over."

"I can think of a few ways I can help you pass the time." Finn pulled her close again. Cupping her face with one hand, he leaned in for another kiss.

Willa thought she'd be too tense to enjoy it. She wasn't.

And when he opened the door to his room, she was more than happy to step inside.

Chapter Fourteen

A T TWENTY MINUTES to four there was a tapping on
Finn's door. Willa was immediately awake, pulling
away from the circle of Finn's warm embrace.

"Who's that?"

"Kris Krinkles," Finn replied, sounding a little groggy.

"Oh, my gosh." This really was going to happen. She
couldn't believe it. Quickly she pulled on her clothes, while
Finn did the same.

Thirty seconds later they opened the door to find a fully-
outfitted Santa standing out in the hall.

"I'm about to wake up your son and invite him on the
adventure," Kris said. "I thought you'd like to listen in."

"Yes," Willa whispered. "But what if he doesn't want to
go? What if he gets scared?"

"You'll be right here to reassure him, in that case."

"Okay," she agreed, reluctantly allowing Finn to close his
door so it was only open a crack.

A few second later, she could hear Kris speaking to her
son. "Merry Christmas, Scout. This is Santa. I'm having a
little trouble tonight and I was wondering if you could help

me."

Willa waited for her son to scream, but he did nothing of the kind.

"What's the matter?"

"It's getting late and I still have a bunch of presents to deliver to the sick children at the hospital. Is there any chance you could help?"

"What about my mom?"

"We won't disturb her. And we'll be back before she wakes up."

"I want to help. But I'm not supposed to go with strangers."

"That's a good rule. Your mother is absolutely right on that."

Willa was so proud of Scout in that moment. Yet she knew she couldn't let this opportunity pass him by. With a nod from Finn, she pulled the door open and slipped into the room.

"Scout," she whispered. "It's Mom. If you want to go help Santa, you can."

"Really? Awesome! Thanks Mom!"

And in the time it took him to slip on his coat, snow pants, boots, hat and mitts, he was gone.

BACK IN FINN'S room, Willa collapsed on the bed. "I can't believe I let him go. I can't believe he wasn't scared."

"Let me tell you a thing about boys. They love adventures."

"In books, maybe."

"In real life, too. Trust me, Scout is going to remember this all his life."

Willa nodded. It did make her proud that Scout cared about the sick children. Having been one himself for far too long, he could certainly relate to their situation.

Finn put his arms around her waist. "Any chance I could convince you to come back to bed?"

She relaxed against his chest. "Tonight was fabulous. But I'm not going to be able to sleep until he's home and safe."

"Who said anything about sleeping?"

She laughed softly. "How about a game of Scrabble instead?"

"Strip Scrabble? In bed?"

"Yes, to the in-bed part."

He planted a soft kiss on her lips. "I'll take what I can get. I'll run downstairs and get the game."

Once he was gone, Willa went to the window, drew back the curtain, and looked out into the dark night. It would be hours before dawn. She hoped Scout and Kris Krinkles wouldn't be gone too long. With a sigh, she dropped the curtain, then made a small circuit of the room. She noticed Finn's sketchbook on the bureau and resisted the urge to look inside. There was a UPS envelope beside it, which she barely glanced at.

But then she took a second look.

Something had caught her eye. Something that didn't seem right.

The name on this envelope was Greg Finnegan Conrad.

She picked up the letter, focusing on the name as if somehow the letters might arrange themselves into something that made sense. But the letters remained in place. Keeping the letter in her hand, she went to the nightstand where Finn had placed his wallet. Gingerly she opened it and pulled out the first card she saw, a credit card.

On the card was the same name. Greg Finnegan Conrad.

Willa couldn't breathe. She blinked several times, almost not trusting her own eyes. This—this just couldn't be real. And yet the card and the letter both felt so solid in her fingers.

Who was this man she'd just slept with—Finn Knightly or Greg Finnegan Conrad?

A moment later she heard Finn quietly enter the room.

"I found it," he said.

She held up the envelope and the Visa. "So did I."

He looked at her stunned.

"Is this your real name?"

"Ah, Willa. You weren't supposed to find out this way."

Despite the evidence, she'd been praying she was wrong, but his words dashed her faint hopes.

"A-are you Greg Conrad's son?"

"I am."

The pain in her heart was so fierce she could hardly

speak. "A-and Finn Knightly…?"

"I've always gone by Finn. Knightly is my mother's maiden name. She liked me using it for my nom de plume. She saw it as a tribute to her father, who was also an artist."

He wasn't one or the other. He was both. "So it's not a coincidence we both ended up in Marietta?"

"No. But does it really matter what brought us to this town? As soon as I met you, I knew you were special. I had no plans to fall in love. I actually fought it. But it happened. And as far as I'm concerned, it's the only thing that matters."

"Love? How can you even talk about love? There is no love without honesty. You didn't have the decency to tell me who you really were, and you expect me to believe you love me?"

"I didn't tell you because I was ashamed. Almost as soon as I met you I realized you weren't the sort of woman who'd swindle money from a sick man."

"Oh, my gosh." She should have seen that coming, but somehow she had not. "You thought I was…that I had…"

A lump grew in her throat. Anger and hurt warred inside her. She didn't know which she felt more strongly. What she did know was that her heart ached and the world was suddenly spinning. She pressed her back against the wall, needing something solid behind her to keep standing.

"I'm so sorry, Willa. But try to see it from my family's point of view. We find out from a lawyer that our father left a nurse he'd only known six weeks fifty thousand dollars.

Can't you see how odd that seemed to us?"

"Of course I can. I certainly would have understood if you'd wanted to talk to me about it." She waved the envelope in front of his face. "So why didn't you just call me and ask me to explain?"

Finn rubbed his jaw, looking troubled, pale. "I was afraid you wouldn't talk to me once you found out who I was."

"Right. Because I had to protect my fifty thousand dollars, right? Let me tell you something, *Greg Finnegan Conrad.* You and your family can have every penny your father bequeathed to me. All I ask in exchange is that you never try to contact me again. And that starts right now."

With that, she dropped the envelope to the ground and ran out of his room.

TEARS FLOODED WILLA'S eyes as she fled out the door to the sanctuary of her room. Logic told her she'd done nothing wrong, but she couldn't help feeling dirty and ashamed. She hadn't asked for, or even wanted that darn fifty thousand dollars! And as for the ring...

She pulled it off and tossed it into the top bureau drawer. It wasn't fair! Greg Conrad had meant for the ring to bring her happiness, but wearing it had brought her nothing but grief.

She thought back to her first days at the B&B, the feeling she'd had that Finn didn't approve of her somehow. And yet, he'd befriended her, specifically so he could worm out her confidences about his father.

And then, if that wasn't enough, he'd courted her and seduced her.

She'd been such an easy mark, never once suspecting he had an ulterior motive.

Willa went to the bathroom and splashed water on her face. Then she stared at her reflection, suddenly angry.

No more guilt. She'd done nothing wrong, except maybe dreaming too big. In her prayers she'd never asked for anything more than Scout's good health and happiness. Her mistake had been reaching for romance and love, as well.

Well, she'd learned her lesson on that score.

Willa paced the confines of the room. It was ten minutes past five now, and still pitch dark outside. She was suffocating in here. But she didn't dare go for a walk and risk missing Scout's return. She couldn't even go down to the sitting room in case she ran into Finn.

Finally, she had a bath and put on her PJs. She'd just finished brushing her teeth, when the door opened and Scout slipped into the dimly lit room.

She turned off the water. "Scout are you all right?"

"Mom! Mom! It was amazing." He was sitting on the floor, tugging off his boots.

"I'm so glad, honey." She hugged him, feeling the cold of the night on his jacket. "Were you warm enough?"

"Yup. I was in a sleigh, Mom, and it was pulled by a team of really nice dogs 'cause the reindeer were busy doing another route."

She could tell he was trying to keep his voice quiet, but his enthusiasm came through loud and clear.

"Real dogs, huh?" She unzipped his jacket, then helped him step out of the snow pants.

"Santa drove us to the hospital and we had to be really quiet. I helped Santa put gifts in the stockings for all the kids. But one girl was awake and crying because she was hurting. And I talked to her and told her about how I used to hurt too, but now I'm better, and maybe she'll be better soon, too."

She led her son to the bathroom where he made quick work of brushing his teeth, going pee and washing his hands.

By the time he hit the bed, his eyes were fluttering closed, but he still kept talking.

"And there were cookies and milk, and Santa shared them with me."

"That was nice."

"Uh huh. And the best part, Mom?"

"What's that Scout?" Despite her broken heart, his happiness made her smile.

"He's real, Mom. There actually is a Santa."

WILLA SLEPT. SHE hadn't expected to. But the sound of Scout's even breathing soothed her and she drifted off for a few hours of sweet oblivion.

Scout, bless his heart, slept in until eight. No sooner had

he awoken though, than he scampered to the end of his bed and came back with a stocking stuffed with goodies.

Willa studied it with disbelief. Her own stocking and gifts for Finn were waiting for him under the tree in the breakfast room.

"You have one too, Mom." Scout retrieved a pretty red stocking decorated with white snowflakes. "Can we open them now?"

"Sure. I guess." Had Kris Krinkles come in while they were sleeping? The idea was a little creepy. Or, looked at another way, kind of magical.

Willa found bath salts, her favorite hand cream—and how could Kris Krinkles have known that?—as well as warm socks, mittens and some of Sage's pistachio truffle balls—again, Willa's favorite.

Befuddled, she set aside her gifts and duly admired Scout's treasures until finally she suggested it was time they put on their robes and go down for breakfast.

Yesterday Eliza had told her that they had a strict PJs only dress code for Christmas morning and that she and Scout could come down at their leisure.

Willa was congratulating herself on keeping it all together, but one glance at Finn's door as they stepped out into the hall almost did her in. Tears blurred her vision and she paused to blink them away.

"Mom, can I check if Finn's up? I want to tell him about last night! It was like an Everyday Sam adventure!"

Willa shook her head. "If he's not at the breakfast table yet, we should let him sleep."

Her heart thudded as they made their way downstairs. Would Finn be there? Would he try to talk to her?

But there was only one person sitting at the table when they entered. From her sour expression it seemed Mable Bramble had not been infected with any Christmas cheer. Nor was she following the PJ dress code. As usual she was wearing a very proper blouse and skirt, her hair pulled back in the rather severe style she favored.

Mable did manage to unbend enough to wish them a Merry Christmas, just as Eliza and Marshall entered the room, both dressed in PJs and robes and carrying platters of bacon and blueberry banana pancakes with whipped cream.

"Yay, bacon, my favorite!"

"Merry Christmas, Scout." Marshall gave Scout a fist bump. "Did Santa come last night?"

"He sure did. We went on a sleigh pulled by dogs. And I helped him get toys to the sick kids too."

Mable sniffed with disapproval, clearly assuming the child was fibbing, but Eliza and Marshall made an appreciative audience.

Scout held court throughout breakfast, sharing the story of his Christmas Eve adventure. Willa sipped coffee and listened, trying not to focus too much on the empty chair where Finn usually sat.

Eventually hunger got the best of Scout, and he gave up

talking in favor of eating.

Willa put a little food on her plate and hoped no one noticed her lack of appetite. But of course Eliza did. Several times she seemed on the verge of saying something to her. Each time though, she stopped.

After his first serving had been gobbled up, Scout asked, "Is Kris Krinkles still in his room? I want to thank him for the presents. And see if maybe we can go for another sleigh ride this afternoon."

"I'm sorry Scout, but he's gone," Eliza said gently. "We won't see him again until next Christmas."

"Oh." Scout took a moment to digest that. "What about Finn?"

Willa held her breath waiting for the answer.

Eliza's gaze shifted to Willa. "Finn went to the Graff for breakfast today. Just for…something different, I guess."

Scout turned to his mom. "Will I get to see him before we go home tomorrow?"

"I'm not sure," Willa said softly, mashing a piece of her pancake with her fork, sensing Eliza's sympathetic eyes on her.

"He's not here," Eliza said. "However he did ask me to give you these." From under the tree she pulled out two rectangular-shaped presents, one wrapped in silver, the other blue. She handed the blue one to Scout.

"Wow, thanks!" Scout lost no time unwrapping his gift, and as soon as he spied what was inside, a smile spread over his face. "Look, Mom, it's a Shane Doan sweater!" Quickly he slipped the hockey jersey over his head.

"Shane Doan?" Eliza asked.

"He's the captain for the Coyotes," Marshall explained. "That's an awesome jersey Scout."

"I can wear it when we go to the game for my birthday."

Willa had already purchased tickets to the hockey game on January twenty-fifth, her son's birthday. Somehow Finn had managed to buy her son the perfect Christmas gift. Which only made her heart ache all the more.

"What did you get, Mom?" Scout was looking at the untouched gift on her lap.

"Oh. Hang on." Slowly she worked the tape from the silver wrapping paper, almost afraid to see what Finn had selected for her. Inside she found a milk chocolate-colored cashmere scarf with matching hat and gloves. The wool was as soft to the touch as a newborn kitten.

The color was almost identical to the sweater she'd been wearing when Finn first kissed her. He'd touched her cheek. *You have amazing skin. That color is perfect on you.*

"Oh darn," Scout said. "I was hoping you got a hockey sweater too."

She'd bought Finn a gift too, of course. She could see it from here, under the tree. Willa had to blink quickly as tears blurred her vision.

Scout came up beside her. "But that's a pretty nice scarf," he said as if trying to buck up her spirits.

"It is," she agreed softly. "Scout would you pass out the gifts we bought for Miss Bramble, Eliza and Marshall? After that you can open the rest of your presents."

"Sure!" Scout played Santa, reading the labels on the wrapped gifts, then handing them out to the appropriate people. Willa had chosen books for Marshall and Eliza, since she knew they both enjoyed reading. But for Mable, she'd had to think a little harder, eventually selecting a vintage tin of her favorite Darjeeling tea.

"This is...perfect. Thank you, dear."

They were the nicest words Willa had heard the woman say during their entire visit. "You're welcome."

Next Scout opened his gifts, exclaiming over the Lego set that Marshall and Eliza had purchased, and politely thanking Mable for the socks. He was thrilled with his new Everyday Sam book, of course. But when he opened his skates, he actually whooped. "Can we go skating right now, Mom?"

"I have a few more gifts to open, honey. And we still need to get dressed."

From Marshall and Eliza, Willa received a print of a local artist's rendering of Copper Mountain. "It's lovely. Thank you so much."

"It was meant to remind you of your time spent in Marietta," Eliza said, her kind eyes uncertain.

"Scout and I have had a wonderful Christmas here," she assured the other woman. "This is the perfect gift."

"Wait 'til you open *mine*, Mom!" Scout pulled out a

package he had clearly wrapped himself, about the size of a small magazine.

Inside, however, was a home-made book. On the cover was a little boy wearing a cape and standing victorious on a hospital bed. The title was written in bold red letters, *Everyday Sam Beats Cancer*. Below the title and the picture the author was listed as Scout Fairchild. In much smaller letters, at the very bottom of the cover, *Illustrated by Finn Knightly*.

"I wrote a book for you, Mom! Finn helped me. And he drew the pictures, too."

"Oh, Scout." Willa's throat threatened to close right over. She gave her son a tight hug, then kissed his cheek. "I'm so proud...of you."

She couldn't say more than that without crying. Instead she held out the book to him.

"Want me to read it to you?"

She nodded.

The story was a simple one. A little boy finds out he has cancer. His daddy goes away. His mommy stays. He is sick a long time. His friends are scared to play with him. He gets better. He becomes an NHL hockey player.

As Scout read, Willa could feel the emotion building in the room. Mable, Eliza, Marshall. None of them had known Scout's story until this moment, when he used his six-year-old words to tell it.

"The end," Scout pronounced proudly, unaware of the

ation he'd just made to the others in the room.

huge revelation he'd just made to the others in the room.

Mable was the first to speak. "My dear boy. That is a wonderful book."

"You're very talented, Scout," Eliza concurred, giving him a hug.

Even Marshall's eyes were tearing up. "That Sam sure is a brave kid."

"And a good hockey player, too," Scout said.

Chapter Fifteen

FINN DIDN'T RETURN to the B&B until after lunch, when he was sure Willa and Scout would be at the lake skating. Christmas carols were playing softly from a speaker in the sitting room. The fire was burning and Ace was in his usual sleeping spot.

He went upstairs to get his laptop. The doors to the White and Red rooms were open, so he could see the beds had been stripped of their linens. He paused for a moment at Willa and Scout's closed door. All seemed quiet inside. They must be out skating as he'd guessed.

The guilt and regret that had kept him awake all night threatened to drown him again. He'd been such an idiot. And why? He had no decent excuse, not even for himself.

Once he had the laptop he went downstairs and found Eliza in the kitchen, chopping up leftover vegetables for her daily batch of homemade soup.

She set down her knife when she heard him come in. "Finally! What in the world happened between you and Willa last night? She looked almost as miserable this morning as you do."

Finn knew he looked rough. He hadn't slept. Hadn't shaved. And hadn't eaten, other than the coffee he'd over-dosed on at the Graff that morning. He sat on a stool on the other side of the butcher block counter. Then he took the envelope from North West DNA Labs from his jeans pocket and slid it over to her.

Eliza looked at it warily. "Is this what I think it is?"

"The results of our DNA test."

"And?"

The letter was unsealed. He'd read it this morning. "Ac-cording to the kinship index, there is a very high probability you and I are related." His voice sounded devoid of anima-tion, which struck him as odd. Because this was pretty major shit. By all rights, he ought to care.

"We are? That's—incredible." Eliza opened the envelope and read the results for herself. Then she shook her head. "You were right. Who would have guessed? I mean, what are the odds?"

"Better than you think," Finn confessed. "I didn't come totally clean with you the other day."

"Oh, boy. Something tells me I'd better sit down for this."

"That's probably wise."

"Does this have anything to do with Willa?"

"It does."

"Oh, no."

"It also involves my sisters, Molly, Keelin and Berneen.

Do you mind if I Skype them in? I'd rather just go through this once."

Eliza put a hand to her hair, which was pulled back into a ponytail.

"You look great," he assured her. And she did. If you discounted the silly sweater she was wearing.

"I wish I could say the same for you."

"Frankly, I couldn't care less how I look." He set his laptop sideways on the counter so both he and Eliza would show up on the camera. Earlier he'd told his sisters he wanted to talk to them without their mother. They were all gathered at Molly's place right now. Their mom was at her sister Betty's for a few hours and Charlie had taken the kids to the park to blow off some steam.

Within sixty seconds they were connected. His sisters were sitting on Molly's family room couch, with Molly in the middle holding the laptop and the other two leaning in.

"Finn? What the hell happened to you?" Berneen was the first one to talk.

"Merry Christmas to you, too," Finn answered, trying not to feel cross. "Keelin, Molly and Berneen, this is Eliza McKenzie. She and her husband run the B&B where I've been staying the past three weeks."

There was a jumble of conversation while everyone said hello at the same time.

"Okay," Finn interrupted. "If everyone will be quiet for a few minutes, I have some major explaining to do. First, to

Eliza. I booked in here using the nom de plume I use as an illustrator, Finn Knightly. But legally I'm Greg Finnegan Conrad."

Eliza looked at him blankly. "Why did you do that?"

"Because Willa Fairchild would have recognized my legal name. The patient who gave her the ring that looks like your great-grandmother's? He was my father, Greg Conrad."

"This doesn't make any sense." Eliza glanced from him to his sisters. All three of them were looking rather sheepish.

"We thought Willa had somehow tricked our father into leaving her that ring—as well as a lot of money," Molly explained. "We didn't know he felt sorry for her because her son had been through leukemia treatments and left her heavily in debt."

"We only found out this morning that Scout had been sick." Eliza turned to Finn and frowned. "So you came here because you thought Willa swindled your father?"

"Something like that," he admitted. "Of course as soon as I got to know her I realized she wasn't that sort of person. But it was too late to tell her my real name by then. She would have been furious. And I—didn't think I could handle that."

"Oh, my God," Molly said. "You've fallen in love with her."

Finn didn't deny it. "Doesn't matter. She hates my guts now."

"Well, who could blame her," Eliza muttered. "I'm sorry,

Finn, but seriously. How could you?"

"Don't blame Finn too much," Keelin said. "Our mother pushed him pretty hard on this."

"As did the three of us," Molly added. "Or at least Berneen and I did. We were pretty shocked that our father would leave so much money to someone he'd only known six weeks."

"I guess that must have seemed odd," Eliza agreed.

"We could have handled the situation a lot smarter. But it's too late now. What we do need to discuss though is what I've learned about Dad's ring. It turns out it was one of four designed for Henry Bramble back in the early nineteen hundreds."

"How did Dad end up with it?" Berneen asked.

"Impossible to say for sure. But my guess is that Grandma Judith had an affair with Henry's great-grandson, Steven Bramble, and our father was the result of that affair."

"So," Eliza continued with his logic, "You believe Steven gave Judith the ring? And that she then gave it to your father?"

"That's right. Maybe in his mind it made up for the fact he wouldn't marry her. Judith must have given Dad the ring when he got married so he could give it to Mom. But she didn't like it and never wore it. Either because it had come to hold too many unhappy memories, or maybe because he couldn't decide which of his daughters to give it to, Dad then gave it to his nurse."

"He sure was fond of her."

"She was nice to him. She spent hours talking to him when he was in pain and couldn't sleep. Plus he felt sorry for her. Willa's had a lot to deal with."

"I'm so glad she was there for Dad, when none of us could be," Molly said softly. "We have a lot to thank her for."

"Agreed." Finn couldn't say more, his emotions were too raw on that subject right now.

He cleared his throat. "As an interesting addendum to this story, a few weeks ago Eliza and I sent samples of our saliva out for DNA testing. I wanted to confirm my hunch that our dad was a Bramble."

Eliza held up the papers she'd just read so his sisters could see them. "And it's true. Your brother and I have DNA that is similar enough to suggest that we're cousins."

There was a burst of overlapping comments from his sisters, who were clearly overwhelmed by the news.

Eliza stepped in at the first pause, "I'm the self-appointed Bramble family historian, so you can imagine how exciting this is for me."

"A whole new branch of the family tree," Keelin said.

"That's right. I'd like you all to consider this your official invite to Marietta, Montana."

They chatted a few minutes longer, mostly his sisters and Eliza exchanging news about each other. Then Molly's husband and kids came home and they had to sign off.

For a while all was quiet in the Bramble kitchen. Playing softly in the background was James Taylor's version of *Go Tell It On The Mountain.*

Eliza started drumming her fingers on the countertop. "I don't know whether to welcome you to the family or bop your head with my wooden spoon."

"I'll take the wooden spoon. I just realized that being welcomed to the family would mean Mable is my aunt, too."

Eliza smiled at this, then she sobered. "And to think I just published our family history. Talk about bad timing."

"Sorry about that."

"I've already wrapped copies of my book for all my cousins for Christmas and it's too late to buy them something else." She sighed. "I'm just going to have to give them the books. Maybe I'll wait until Boxing Day to tell them the book is missing some major plot twists. Unless, you want to come for Christmas and meet your new cousins?"

He rubbed his chin, feeling the stubble. He might not be looking his best right now...but it was still a lot prettier than the way he felt inside.

"I'd like to meet them sometime. But not this trip."

IN THE END, Finn couldn't keep away from Willa and Scout entirely. It was mid-afternoon as he rounded the bend for the final approach to Miracle Lake. Though the sun had been shining all day, white crystals of hoarfrost still clung to the branches of the trees, making a dazzling contrast against the sapphire-blue sky.

About twenty people were out skating, and at least that number again were standing around the bonfire sipping hot cocoas or rubbing their hands.

It was a cheerful, colorful picture, and on instinct he reached for his Nikon. But he hadn't brought his camera with him this time.

It didn't take long to spot the number nineteen Coyotes jersey he'd bought for Scout. The young boy was zipping around the ice like an old pro. The taller girl beside him— Savannah, Finn thought—seemed to be having trouble keeping up.

A few seconds later he saw Willa doing slower laps around the lake with Sage. She wasn't wearing the scarf he'd bought her, but she had on the skates that had been wrapped under the tree and labeled 'To: Willa, From: Santa.' Guess she hadn't figured out they were from him, too, or she probably wouldn't be wearing them either.

Finn sat on a wooden bench close to the trees at the far south side of the lake, well apart from the crowd. He was glad to see Scout was in high spirits. He couldn't read Willa's mood, though. She was in an animated conversation with Sage, too engrossed to even notice him.

Which was fine.

He hadn't come here to talk. He knew he had no right to ask that of her. He'd just needed to see them, to know they were having a nice Christmas. Because after all they'd been

A BRAMBLE HOUSE CHRISTMAS

through they deserved that much.

Eventually he'd have to find a way to convince Willa to keep his dad's money. He couldn't let his foolish actions unravel his father's last act of kindness. But since the will was still in probate, he had time for that.

Finn was standing, preparing to leave, when Scout suddenly spotted him.

"Hey! Finn!" The little boy broke away from the crowd and skated to the other end of the lake, coming right to the edge closest to Finn. "Thanks for my sweater! How did you know Shane Doan is my favorite player?"

"Lucky guess. Looks good on you, buddy."

"Did you bring your skates?"

"No...I just wanted to say good-bye since we're both going home tomorrow."

"Aren't you coming for Christmas dinner?"

"Uh—don't think so sport." When they'd made their reservation a week ago, that had been the plan. But now Finn was prepared to settle for a bowl of Eliza's homemade soup. Maybe he'd catch a movie after that.

Hopefully the local theater wasn't still playing *It's a Wonderful Life*. Finn didn't think he could handle watching it ever again.

Willa must have noticed him, because she was skating toward them now.

Judging by her expression, she wasn't pleased that he was here. Finn would have obliged her and left, but Scout was

197

still talking to him.

"Mom really liked the book we made her."

By now Willa was close enough to hear. "Yes. It's a great book. Thanks for helping Scout with that."

The words were polite, but her tone had a frosty edge meant to put him in his place and keep him there.

Finn swallowed. None of this was made easier by the fact that she looked fantastic. Her gorgeous chestnut hair framed her face in soft curls. And her ivory skin glowed as if she'd had the best night's sleep of her life, which he kind of doubted.

He took a backward step. "It was a fun project. Scout, if you ever want a break from the NHL, you can write children's books for a living."

"Maybe we can be partners again," Scout said hopefully.

Willa went behind her son and placed her hands on his shoulders. "You better say good-bye, honey. I don't think we'll see Finn again before we leave."

In other words, she didn't *want* to see him. Which was what Finn had expected.

But hearing her say the words broke his heart, all the same.

He turned to oblige her, and get out of her life as quickly as possible.

Then at the last moment he decided there was something he wanted to say. Though Scout had skated off, she was still standing there. Some of the ice had left her eyes. When she blinked, even though he was too far away to see them, he knew she had tears in her eyes.

"I just thought you should know that the envelope you saw last night had the results of a DNA test comparing my DNA with Eliza's. Turns out we're cousins."

The news seemed to stun her. "Do you think your father knew?"

"I wish he had. But, no, I don't think so."

After a moment she nodded. "Well. Thanks for telling me that."

He tried like crazy to think of a way to prolong their conversation, but she was already skating away.

Chapter Sixteen

CHRISTMAS DINNER AT the beautiful historic Graff Hotel was a scrumptious six-course affair, but the fine food was wasted on Willa and Scout.

She still had almost no appetite. And Scout was no gourmet. He eschewed the chestnut soup and roasted acorn squash salad for extra rolls and butter. And the orange and cranberry glazed Cornish game hens just puzzled him.

"I wish we could have some of Grandma's turkey."

"This is sort of like turkey. Let me cut it up for you." But, she too suddenly found herself homesick for her mom and dad and their unvarying holiday menu—served for Easter, Christmas and Thanksgiving—of turkey and mashed potatoes, sweet potato pie and broccoli cheese casserole.

Even as she missed them, though, she did not look forward to flying home tomorrow.

The condo in her parents' gated community had been wonderfully practical and convenient when Scout was ill.

But it had never felt like home. All their neighbors were over fifty and Scout's school was a thirty minute drive away.

There were many nice family-oriented communities in

Phoenix, and now that Scout was healthy there was lots to explore in Arizona. But this town had a special aura, a vibrancy and a warmth. The people were friendly—well, except for Aunt Mable—and the surrounding ranchlands and mountains had an in-your-face beauty that continually made her catch her breath. She was even becoming a fan of winter. It certainly suited her son and his love of skating and hockey.

This afternoon, when she'd confessed to Sage how much she was dreading going back to Phoenix, Sage had said, "Why don't you move here? You'd love living in Marietta. And you already have friends."

It had been such a sweet thing to say, and it was certainly true that Sage and her family, as well as Eliza and Marshall, already felt like friends she'd known all her life.

But until she paid off her loans, she couldn't afford to move anywhere. And now that she'd refused Greg Conrad's bequest, it was going to take twice as long to get her accounts in the black.

Not that she regretted throwing that money back in Finn's face. She couldn't abide having Greg Conrad's family thinking of her as some sort of scam artist.

WHEN THEY RETURNED to the B&B after a scrumptious dessert offering of pumpkin pie, chocolate mousse or a modern twist on Baked Alaska, Finn was already in his room.

"Can I knock on his door to say goodnight?" Scout asked.

"No. He might be sleeping."

"But his light is on. Look." Scout pointed at the thin gap where the door didn't quite meet the carpeted floor.

"He could still be in bed. Which is where we should be."

Later, as she tucked her tired son under his covers he yawned.

"It was the best Christmas ever. Wasn't it, Mom?"

Willa gave her son a smile. Hearing him say those words made everything she'd been through worthwhile. "It sure was, son.

He touched her face the way he often had done when he was younger. "Then why do you look sad?"

She tried to swallow the sudden blockage at her throat. Her dear son was much too perceptive. "Because we have to leave tomorrow."

"Yeah. I'm sad about that, too."

Willa squeezed in beside him on the small bed and read aloud his new *Everyday Sam* book—three times, on request. Halfway through the third reading, he fell asleep. Slowly she crept out of his bed, and crawled into her own.

After a last, reassuring glance at her sleeping son, she turned out the light.

Why do you look sad?

Scout's words kept playing in her mind. And the more she thought about how miserable she felt, the more she had to face the truth. Marietta was a lovely town. But it was leaving Finn that was breaking her heart.

Willa spread out in the large bed, remembering how difficult it had been to adjust to sleeping alone after Jeff left. Whenever Scout wasn't in hospital, she'd encourage him to sleep with her. Partly to be there to comfort him if he woke up hurting or afraid.

But her son's presence had comforted her, too. She'd filled the gaping hole Jeff had left in her life, with caring for and protecting their son. It had taken meeting Finn for her to realize all she was missing.

He'd slipped into her heart so easily, not the least because he was so awesome with her son. Being with him just felt right. Finn was steady, rock solid and kind. And yet, he was so much fun, as well. She hadn't laughed as much in three years as she had these past three weeks.

And what had she done after meeting this great guy?

She'd pushed him away.

A sob pushed up from her heart, and she pressed her face into the pillow to muffle the sound.

Yes, Finn had deceived her. But he'd been trying to protect his family and grieving over his father. Hadn't she deceived him, too, by withholding the truth about Scout's cancer? And she'd done that for similar reasons. To protect Scout.

Willa could feel the tears streaming down her cheeks, dampening the pillow. She gave into her need to cry quietly, so as not to disturb her son. It was something she had a lot of practice at.

THE NEXT MORNING Willa and Scout found only Eliza waiting for them at the breakfast table. She'd put out fruit salad, muffins and boiled eggs.

"I hope you don't mind that we're keeping things simple this morning."

"It's perfect." Willa went straight for the coffee. She wasn't sure how much longer she could run on coffee and adrenaline. Given the drive ahead of her, she supposed she'd better force down a little bit of food. "Where's your aunt?"

"She's exhausted after our dinner at the Circle C last night. It was pretty chaotic."

"I hope she isn't ill."

"No, she just craved quiet, so she's having tea and toast in the library. Marshall ate earlier so he could take the day off and go skiing. Patricia and Mike booked out an hour ago and…Finn is eating at the diner this morning."

Willa sighed. Then seeing the sympathy in Eliza's eyes, quickly changed the subject. "So did your cousins like your book?"

"They did. I haven't yet told them about the new branch of the family tree though—" Abruptly she went quiet, as if worried she'd said something wrong.

"It's okay. Finn told me about the DNA test. I guess in a way it's lucky he followed me here, or you might never have found out the truth."

"Willa, can I just say how sorry I am? I totally understand how hurt and upset you must feel. But, it just seems like such a shame how things ended. You and Finn were getting along so well."

Willa glanced at her son, thankful to see him picking out cranberries from his muffins, apparently oblivious to what they were discussing.

"Yes, we were. Perhaps I—overreacted. I just felt so betrayed. I must have spoken about my patient, Greg Conrad, dozens of times over the three weeks, without the slightest idea I was speaking to his son."

Eliza nodded sadly. "Yes. That was very deceptive."

Determined to change the subject, Willa asked, "So do you have any new guests coming in this week?"

"We're actually closed for three days, opening again in time for New Year's. Marshall and I plan to get away for some skiing at Baker Creek Cabins. It's where we first met."

"That sounds lovely. Thank you so much for everything, Eliza. Scout and I have really enjoyed staying here."

"I hope you'll come back sometime."

"Maybe." But Willa knew, without Finn, that would never happen.

FINN STILL HADN'T made an appearance by the time Willa had their suitcases packed and waiting at the door. It really was time to leave. She just had one last thing to do.

"Wait here, Scout."

Her son glanced at the plate of leftover Christmas cookies. "Is it okay if I have one more cookie?"

"Sure. I'll be right back."

She knocked on the library door, and when she heard a reluctant, "Yes?" walked in.

Mable Bramble was sitting in her favorite chair, properly dressed and reading one of the books she'd no doubt received as a gift that Christmas.

"Willa. What is it?"

"Sorry to interrupt Miss Bramble. We're just about to leave and I had to give you something."

"Your Christmas gift yesterday was quite sufficient. I hope you and your son have a safe journey."

"Since finding out that this ring is a Bramble heirloom, I don't feel right wearing it." She passed the sapphire ring to the elderly woman.

Mable peered at her sternly. "Are you sure? It's quite valuable. It seems that you and your son could use the money."

"I could never sell it. And I simply can't keep it, either. Not now that I know where it really belongs."

"Well. That's very generous of you, my dear."

"It's the right thing."

Back in the foyer she found Scout reaching for a second cookie. As soon as he saw her, he withdrew his hand.

She gave him a sharp look. "How about you take an apple for the road in case you get the munchies."

"I guess Christmas really is over," he said despondently.

Willa took one last look at the sitting room, her gaze falling on the empty chair by the fire, Finn's favorite. "Yes. I'm afraid it is."

FINN DRANK SO many cups of coffee in the diner, his head began to buzz. Finally, when he was certain Willa and Scout would be on the road to Bozeman, he walked back to the B&B to pack for his own flight, later that afternoon. He'd no sooner opened the door than he heard Mable Bramble calling his name.

The door to the library was open. She frowned at him, then waved him inside.

"What's kept you young man? I've been waiting forever."

"Did we have an appointment?"

"Of course not you silly oaf." She picked something up from the table and handed it to him.

It was Willa's ring. He looked up in surprise. "Where did you get this?"

"She gave it to me. Some nonsense about it belonging in the Bramble family."

That sounded like Willa. "What do you want me to do? Her car is gone, she's already enroute to the airport."

Mable shook her head at him. "My dear boy. Do you think chances for love and happiness come along all the time? Most people are lucky if it happens once. And if they are foolish enough to let the chance slip through their fingers, then they have only themselves to blame if they end up alone and bitter."

"You're preaching to the choir, Aunt Mable. I know I'll never meet anyone else like Willa."

"Then what on earth are you doing standing here?"

"But the ring...?"

"Do I have to explain *everything*? Clearly that ring is meant for one person, and only one person. And it certainly isn't me."

FORTUNATELY THE WEATHER conditions were much better for Willa's return trip to Bozeman than they'd been for her arrival, because the way her eyes kept tearing up, she never would have been able to see the roads in a snow storm.

At the airport she returned the rental car, then got a cart and loaded up their luggage. Scout seemed in a cheerful mood, but as they were waiting for their boarding passes to print, he gave a long sigh.

"I wish we didn't have to go, Mom."

"You liked Marietta?"

"Yeah."

Me, too.

"Can we go back next Christmas?"

"Maybe next year we'll visit Aunt Thea in Boston. They get lots of snow in Boston."

"I guess. But I'll miss Savannah. She's pretty cool. And Finn."

"Finn," Willa repeated slowly, wondering if she was seeing things.

Because a man looking just like him had just walked into the airport. He had dark, thick hair like Finn's, hair that always sat perfectly in place even when it was snowing and the wind was howling.

And he had the same smile, the one that was sweet and sexy all at the same time.

Finally, and most importantly, he was looking at her as if he knew her.

No. Not as if he knew her.

As if he loved her.

Willa grabbed hard onto the handle of her luggage cart. The security line was backed-up. If she and Scout didn't hurry, they could miss their flight.

But as Finn drew closer, she didn't turn away. Finally Scout noticed, too, and only then was she certain the man wasn't a figment of her over-stressed and exhausted mind.

"Finn! It's me, Scout!" Her son barreled right at him, wrapping his arms around Finn in a big hug.

Finn crouched to his level. "I was hoping to talk to your mom before you got on your plane."

Scout took his hand. "She's right here."

Willa inhaled deeply, so, so glad she had the luggage cart to hold on to. Finn stopped a mere foot away from her.

"I don't know what I can say to convince you how sorry I am. All I can say in my defense is that I am not a man prone to either lying or deception. In fact, generally, I'm a pretty upstanding guy."

"I believe you," she said softly.

"I came to Marietta for all the wrong reasons, but meeting you has changed all my preconceptions. You're the kind of woman who brings joy to the people around you. I'm so grateful you were there to nurse my father in his final days. Thank you for that, Willa."

She was moved by the sorrow she saw in his eyes. "His final passing was easy, Finn. He just…slipped away."

Relief and tears mingled in Finn's eyes. "Th-that's a relief to hear. My dad was a good guy. Which is why you have to accept the money he left for you. I never cared about it, anyway. I was just hurt that you were the one with him at the end—and not me."

Suddenly she had the strength to let go of the cart and reach for his hand. She squeezed hard. "You didn't let him down, you know."

He held tight to her hand, locking his gaze with hers. "I hope not. But what about you?"

"You didn't let me down, either. I was hurt and shocked when I learned the truth about you. But I do understand your motivations. And I'm sorry I wasn't open about Scout's illness. That was something I should have shared with you as—as we got closer."

Finn pulled something from his pocket. The next moment he was sliding the Bramble ring onto her finger. "My father gave this to you for a reason. Please honor his memory and wear it."

"Oh, Finn…"

"Even Aunt Mable believes this ring was meant for you. I'm hoping the same can be said for me. That my mistake won't stand in the way of what could be an amazing future."

"What mistake?" Scout wanted to know.

Relief and joy comingled in Willa, as she turned to her son. "We're trying to have a grown-up conversation, honey."

"I hate those."

"I know." She glanced around, and spotted a little shop. "Come with me. Why don't you pick out some gum and a snack for the plane ride. Finn and I will be right here, in full sight, waiting for you."

"Does it have to be sugar-free?"

Willa rolled her eyes. "Yes."

Once Scout was out of earshot, Finn took her hand again.

"Willa, I love you. I'm thirty-two years old and I've never felt like this about a woman. Come to Boulder with me for New Year's."

Everything was happening so fast she could hardly breathe. "Do you mean right now?"

"Yes. Now. Today."

"But—" She couldn't think of one objection. Their suitcases were packed with winter appropriate clothing, which she would be able to wash at his place.

More importantly, she wanted to be with him.

"What happens if I say yes?"

Hope grew in his eyes. He took her other hand and pulled her closer. "We'll have a fabulous time. We'll ski and I'll cook for you. I have a fabulous outdoor hot tub. You wouldn't believe all the stars you can see at night."

"And then, when the holiday is over?"

"I'll ask you to marry me. And if you say yes, I'll be like a second dad to Scout. Only this dad would never leave him. Or you. I promise."

She stared into his eyes, feeling the power of his love. It lifted her, filling her with happiness and hope.

And then he kissed her and the final traces of hurt and fear were gone, like helium balloons released into the sky.

"I love you," he said again.

She thought of all the good things that had happened during the past three weeks in Marietta. So much of it was due to Finn. He'd helped her and Scout learn to have fun again. And he'd offered them a strong shoulder when they needed it, too.

"I do love you, Finn."

"So you'll come?"

"I think I have to. I'm pretty sure we've missed our flight."

Green lights danced in his eyes. "That was my strategy. I'm glad it worked."

Suddenly the chorus of Willa's favorite carol popped into

her head. She thought she was hearing things, until she realized music was coming from the speakers in the gift shop...

Oh, tidings of comfort and joy
Comfort and joy
Oh, tidings of comfort and joy!

The End

The Carrigans of Circle C

Hawksley Carrigan, owner of the Circle C Ranch south of Marietta, Montana, always wanted a son to carry on the family name. Unfortunately for him, he ended up with four daughters.

Book 1: Promise Me, Cowboy

Sage Carrigan's story

Book 2: Good Together

Mattie Carrigan's story

Book 3: Close to Her Heart

Dani Carrigan's story

Book 4: Snowbound in Montana

Eliza Bramble's story

Book 5: A Cowgirl's Christmas

Callan Carrigan's story

Available now at your favorite online retailer!

About the Author

USA Today Bestselling author C. J. Carmichael has written over 45 novels in her favorite genres of romance and mystery. She has been nominated twice for the *Romance Writers of America* RITA Award, as well as *RT Bookclub's* Career Achievement in Romantic Suspense award, and the *Bookseller's Best* honor.

She gave up the thrills of income tax forms and double entry book-keeping in 1998 when she sold her first book to Harlequin Superromance. Since then she has published over 35 novels with Harlequin and is currently working on a series of western romances with Tule Publishing. In addition C. J. Carmichael has published several cozy mystery series as an Indie author.

When not writing C. J. enjoys family time with her grown daughters and her husband. Family dinners are great. Even better are the times they spend hiking in the Rocky Mountains around their home in Calgary, and relaxing at their cottage on Flathead Lake, Montana.

Visit C.J.'s website at www.CJCarmichael.com

Thank you for reading

A Bramble House Christmas

If you enjoyed this book, you can find more from all our great authors at TulePublishing.com, or from your favorite online retailer.

TULE
PUBLISHING